Dale Mayer

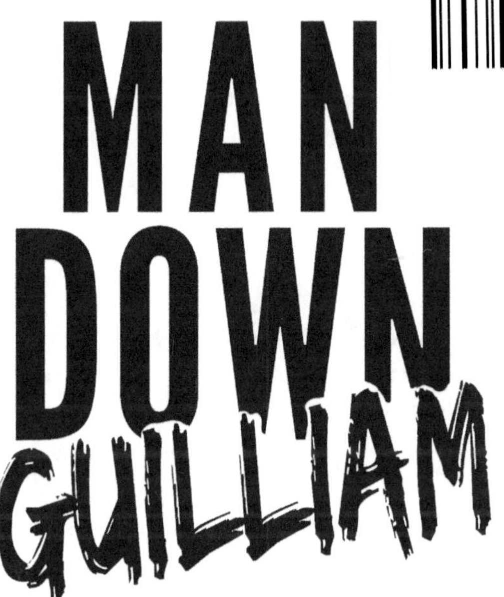

GUILLIAM: MAN DOWN, BOOK 5
Beverly Dale Mayer
Valley Publishing Ltd.

ISBN-13: 978-1-778866-06-7
Print Edition

Books in This Series:

Jasper, Book 1

Masters, Book 2

Gideon, Book 3

Tristan, Book 4

Guilliam, Book 5

Mason's Mark, Book 6

About This Book

There is no greater motive than bloodlust, DNA, and revenge mixed up in a cocktail of hatred …

Guilliam watched his long-term relationship dissolve, and, to a certain extent, he understood it. He knew when the time was right, he would try again. He didn't expect to see her immediately upon arrival at the hospital though, as he joined Jasper's investigation team.

Janelle walked away from Guilliam to nurse her sick mother. It was supposed to be temporary, but the cancer was deadly, and Janelle now remains in the hospital room, knowing this is her mother's last days. Finding out Guilliam was here helped, but knowing he was involved in something deadly had her feeling like she was being watched all the time.

It takes everyone to get to the bottom of this nightmare, but not before it gets way worse …

Sign up to be notified of all Dale's releases here!
https://geni.us/DaleNews

PROLOGUE

GUILLIAM LAFRANKO STEPPED into the hospital and located the room number Tesla had given him. He made an ever-so-slight knock before stepping inside.

She looked up, blanked out for just a moment, then stood up and threw her arms around him. "You came," she cried out.

He hugged her closely. "Of course I did," he murmured, as he looked over at the friend he'd known for so long and sighed. "I sure don't enjoy seeing him like this."

"He won't enjoy your seeing him like this either," she admitted.

"Understood," Guilliam replied, with a nod. "Warriors should always be on their feet, never like this." He looked back at her and asked, "The men, have they found anything?"

"Lots," she admitted, "just not enough."

"It's always that way," he noted. "I'll go find them."

"I haven't told them you were coming."

He waved his hand. "I contacted Jasper, so he knows I'm here."

"Oh good, I wasn't sure how he would take it."

"It doesn't matter how he takes it," he replied, smiling at

her. "All that matters is that we get the job done." He took another close look at his longtime friend Mason and asked, "He's conscious, no?"

"He has been, yes. He manages a few minutes, recognizes me, then goes back under."

"That's good," he noted. "You don't want to push him for more than that right now. If he understood what was going on out there, he would fight to stay conscious, and then he wouldn't heal."

She stared at Guilliam and then nodded. "That's very true. I have to remember that."

"Temporarily you need to look after yourself and the baby and Sebastian, without Mason's help, while Mason looks after himself, despite his condition."

"I hear you," she muttered. "It's just been so terribly hard to sit here and to wait."

"It won't be much longer," he stated. "Hopefully we'll solve this before he wakes up permanently." He gave her a gentle hug and a kiss on the cheek. "You stay here, where it's safe."

"How did you get past the guard?"

"The guard knows me," he said, with a smile, "at least he did once he recognized me. Most people don't recognize me right off the bat. I do that on purpose, but I knew who the guard was on duty right now, so it's all good."

"As long as nobody else can pull that trick."

"No, nobody else will pull that trick. I promise. Do you need anything?"

"No," she whispered, her voice wavering a bit, as she touched her swollen belly. "I just need Mason back."

"He's alive. He's fighting to come back to you. He's waking up occasionally to remind us that he's still in there, fighting. Solving the case and keeping everybody safe in the meantime is up to us."

She nodded. "Do you need anything?"

He smiled. "No, I'm fine." Then studying her for a moment, he asked, "What's up, Tesla?"

She hesitated. "It's just that … Janelle is here."

He raised an eyebrow, as he contemplated Tesla. "Looking after Mason?"

"No, it's her mother. She's a patient here and in a pretty bad way."

He froze, and a sad look entered his gaze. "I'm so sorry to hear that. … Janelle's always been very close to her mother."

"And to you," Tesla pointed out.

"And to me," he confirmed, "but it just wasn't our time. This isn't the time either," he stated, looking at her sternly. "No matchmaking."

She smiled. "I'm not matchmaking. I'm just telling you that she's here, in case you want to see her."

"I'll see," he replied. "Is she working at this hospital?"

"Sometimes. She comes and goes."

"Of course, and her mom is here?"

Tesla shrugged. "Yes, and it sounds like she may not have too long."

He winced. "All right, I'll, … I'll see about contacting her." As he walked away from Tesla and Mason, Guilliam knew he couldn't see Janelle—or her mother. If ever you had loved and lost that one special woman in your life, you sure as hell didn't want to go through such pain again. As he headed down the hallway to the stairs, a woman called out to him.

"Guilliam?"

He froze and turned to look, as Janelle walked toward him. "Janelle," he said, with a smile. "How are you?"

"I'm fine. How are you?" Her words were barely more than a whisper, and her face was pale with shock. "I never expected to see you."

"I can't say that I planned to be here, but *Mason*," he said, with a nod toward his room.

She winced and nodded. "That makes sense. If ever somebody would bring you back here, it would be him."

He hesitated before he added, "Tesla told me about your mother."

Janelle stiffened at first, then slowly relaxed. "Honestly, at this point, her passing will be a blessing," she admitted. "Watching her suffer is pretty hard to take, but it won't be long now."

"I'm so sorry."

She shrugged. "It will be a good thing for Mom."

"In that case, … I hope for an easy passing," he said, as he inched away.

As she headed toward her mother's room, avoiding any more discussion with Guilliam, she called back, "Were you going to contact me?"

He looked up at her and schooled his features. "I just arrived. I didn't know you were here, not until Tesla mentioned it."

"Your head may not have known," she stated, "but your heart would have."

And, with that comment, he knew that any pretense would be completely useless. "I might have looked you up once I realized just what the lay of the land was. My first focus has been on Mason."

"Of course," she replied, a little more formally. "Still, if you can spare a few minutes at some point, it would be nice to spend some time with you."

He stiffened, knowing that spending time with her, although it was everything he'd always wanted, would also be terribly painful for him to endure.

She cut away his unspoken protest and added, "A lot of heartache remains between us, but I would very much like to heal that pain."

He groaned. "I'm not sure that healing for you is the same as for me."

"Maybe not," she whispered, "but it might help us both to spend some time to find out."

He searched her features. "This is new territory for me, so I don't know what to say."

She nodded. "Me too. Nothing like watching somebody dying to make you realize that other decisions you've made may not have been the best." He winced at that, and she nodded. "I hurt you, and I didn't mean to, and I hurt myself as well," she admitted, with a sigh. "I thought I was doing the right thing because my mother needed me."

"She did need you," he confirmed, "and, of course, you had to come help her."

"I did, and you're right, but I didn't have to tear apart what we had. I, … I don't know what I was thinking, or why I did what I did."

His phone went off at that moment, like a lifesaver, and he nodded. "We'll talk. Beyond that, no promises. I have to go."

And, with that, he bolted down the stairs to get out of the hospital and to get away from his past as quickly as he could. One thing he had learned a long time ago was that you could never go back to the way things had been before.

Still, a tiny voice in the back of his head whispered that maybe he didn't have to go back to that. Maybe, just maybe, something better was ahead.

CHAPTER 1

GUILLIAM WALKED INTO the navy's investigation department and stopped at the doorway to Jasper's private office.

Jasper looked up and grinned. "There's a sight for sore eyes." He hopped up and came around.

The two men bro-hugged, and, with the noise of the greetings, the others gathered to see what was going on. Guilliam turned and smiled at Masters, reaching out to shake his hand. When Guilliam saw Gideon, his arms went wide open. With lots of laughter, the four men gathered around. He looked to see a couple others standing off to the side.

"More team members?" he asked, as he walked over and shook their hands. "I'm Guilliam," he murmured. "Nice to meet you."

One of the men glared at him.

Another shrugged and pointed to the glaring guy with him. "We were part of the original investigation team. Not exactly sure what we are at this point, after the MPs locked up Morgan. I'm Lichen, and that's Sam." They both promptly walked off.

Guilliam's eyebrows shot up at that. You could expect

trouble when you came into these investigations in progress, especially if the members weren't all in sync. Guilliam returned to Jasper's office, sat down, and noted, "There is dissent among the natives."

Jasper nodded, along with Masters and Gideon. "There absolutely is, but most of these natives won't be around long enough for me to give a crap."

Guilliam raised an eyebrow. "What is it? Are they bad, incompetent? What's the problem?"

Jasper shrugged, with a nod toward the open door of his office. "It's more than I want to get into right now." Then he looked over at Guilliam. "I presume you've been to the hospital."

"I have. First stop."

"And did you see … Was Mason awake?"

"No, he wasn't, but Tesla was, so I spent a few minutes with her." He frowned. "She's pretty stressed." A note of accusation filled his tone, as he looked over at his friend. "We need to solve this and solve it fast."

"Oh, I agree," Jasper replied. "A shitshow of other events is happening at the same time."

Guilliam nodded. "Fill me in."

Tristan now joined the rest of Jasper's team and shut the door behind him.

Jasper snapped at Tristan. "Why are you here? You need time off, so take it. Then come back so your other team members can have their downtime as well."

Tristan groaned. "I wanted to be here for the update at least."

"Fine," Jasper grumbled, "then off you go."

Guilliam listened as first Jasper, then Masters, Gideon, and Tristan filled him in on the various issues up until now.

"And Nicholas?" Guilliam asked. "Surely we can get more information from him, right?"

"He was held and tortured for four months," Gideon shared. "I'm not sure he'll give us anything in the near future. You know how it is. Our mind shuts down to handle the trauma. The memories fade. Sometimes they come back. Sometimes they don't. There hasn't been any surfacing so far, and we can't push the process. It must be organic."

Guilliam frowned at that, tapping his fingers on his knee as he contemplated the situation. "What's next then?"

"The sniper and his girlfriend are accounted for. We have several visitors in our jail cells at the moment. Some are talking. Some are not. We're verifying the information we're getting on various people, basically finding associations and other potential connections between these people, whether dead or alive, all to figure out who hired the sniper in the first place. And, of course, the USB key held by Drew contains a lot of blackmailable material that gives us more suspects. Unfortunately these weak points to be utilized by our mastermind, or others of that ilk, are mostly in the navy and reside on base."

Guilliam blew out a long breath. "And the sniper is dead, correct? I heard the fake death-by-suicide attempt was followed up by finding his real body, sporting a bullet between the eyes."

They all nodded.

"Good. Well, not good, but, yeah, you know what I mean."

"Exactly," Jasper agreed. "We're not looking at anybody else as the one who pulled the trigger. However, we also don't know whether the shooting was a good one or not."

Guilliam stopped to consider that and nodded. "Right,

that makes sense too. Was missing a deliberate act? Depends, I guess, on how good a shooter Drew was."

"One of the navy's best snipers, according to his military record," Jasper shared.

Guilliam frowned. "So then, we must assume that it was an intentional miss."

"But bad shots do happen," Masters pointed out, "even for the best of us, just not very often. In Mason's shooting, the pressure would have been immense."

"Was it a windy day?"

"It was, so we don't have a clear-cut answer on whether it was a good shooting or not."

"Right, but still not the main issue," Guilliam concluded. "Drew took the job for some reason and was planning to run afterward because he knew perfectly well that somebody was sure to track him down."

"That's what I think," Gideon agreed.

"Have you gotten anywhere on all of the cross-referencing yet?" Guilliam asked.

Jasper shook his head. "Still in progress. So far no leads."

Guilliam frowned. "There has to be something."

"Of course. There always is."

"And yet we're struggling to find anything definitive. You've gone over Mason's past cases?"

"Tesla has been going over a bunch we shortlisted, but, so far, nothing to connect directly to the assassination attempt."

Guilliam shook his head at that. "She shouldn't be involved."

"Yeah, right. I agree," Jasper replied, with a smirk. "Have you had any luck telling her what she should or should not be involved in?"

Guilliam burst out laughing at that. "Okay, that's a very good point. Plus, with her being pregnant, she's in major protective mama-bear mode. Regardless, we need to sort out what the next step is." And he pondered that a second. "I'm thinking I'll take a trip to the site. I know nothing is still around, as far as the crime scenes goes, but I just want to make sure we've covered every base."

The men just nodded.

"I can take you over," Gideon offered.

Guilliam agreed. "Sounds good to me." He stood up and looked back at Jasper. "Did you check the banking on the suspects to date?"

He nodded. "Yes, and we found a couple irregularities. One large payment was made recently."

"Large payments are good," Guilliam stated, with a smile. "You just need to know where it came from."

"Canary Islands."

He wrinkled up his nose. "Which was probably where Drew was running to then."

"That would make sense. Not necessarily the best place for him to go, if you think about it, but—"

"And not a bad place either," Guilliam pointed out, as he considered it. "There will always be people looking to go someplace like that."

"Sure, but we're just not certain that's where the man behind all this might have gone. And Drew didn't have airline tickets booked."

"Not even under another name?" Guilliam asked.

"If he did, we don't have that other name."

"Right. Dammit. You guys been to Drew's house yet?"

They nodded.

Masters added, "Forensics was still working on it, and

they wouldn't let us in."

"They'll let me in," Guilliam declared, with a smile. "Mostly because they won't know." He looked over at Gideon. "You okay to make a stop there as well?"

"Sure, I want in there too."

"Good enough." He pointed toward the door. "Let's go." With that, Guilliam got up and walked over to the huge whiteboard, holding a lot of the information regarding Mason's case. Guilliam took several photos and then nodded. "I'll study this a little bit later," he murmured.

With that, he nodded at Gideon, and the two of them walked out.

JANELLE PACKERS WALKED back to her mother's hospital bed. Out loud she murmured to herself, "Well, Tesla, I knew it wouldn't work. He just doesn't want to see me. Of course I may have jumped the gun, being so excited to see him, but he wasn't of the same opinion, at least not at first glance. Maybe he'll change his mind a little bit later." Yet Janelle wasn't so sure.

When her phone rang, she looked down to see it was Tesla. "Yes, I saw him," she began. "Can't say he looked terribly happy about it, though."

"He just found out you were here," Tesla reminded her. "You'll have to give him a little bit of adjustment time."

"Not sure I'm up for giving him too much time," she stated in a dry tone. "This is me, after all. Remember?"

"I know. However, let's not forget that this is Guilliam, and he's been through a lot too."

"I understand, but now I'm at the end of my mother's

illness. In a way, it, … well, it would have been better if I'd met him in another couple months."

"Life is not that easy," Tesla murmured. "You know that."

"I do know that. I was just hoping that maybe, for once, it would be easy."

"Easy?" Tesla chuckled. "How are you doing? How is your mom?"

"She's okay. I thought moving her back home might bring her some joy, just in getting her away from the treatment facility and her specialist, which only reminded her of her cancer. That trip was hard on her, but I thought she perked up once she knew where she was again. Unfortunately that was a short-lived stay and she's back in the hospital," Janelle sighed loudly. "Maybe all that didn't matter. I mean, she's unconscious and hopefully not in pain, yet clearly nearing the end. They're trying to get her moved to a hospice facility, but we're having an issue finding a place with an opening."

"Of course. That's been an ongoing problem recently. It seems as if everyone is having more than their fair share of challenges lately," Tesla noted. "Hopefully it won't be too long, and that will get resolved, and they'll get her moved and settled."

"Right. Still, she's being well cared for right here."

"Absolutely," Tesla agreed. "Back to Guilliam, give him a break. He was head over heels."

"He was. It's the past tense part that's important to remember."

"Just think of it as not being the right time back then."

Long after she hung up with Tesla, Janelle wondered if it could be that easy. Would Guilliam even think of that, or would it seem like something completely different in his mind? She'd hurt him and had hurt him badly. She knew that. Yet, at the time, her focus had been on her mother and not on him. However, he was right about one thing. Janelle didn't have to discard the one good thing she had going for her just because her mother's health had deteriorated. There should have been a way to keep the good, while dealing with the bad.

Back then she just hadn't been able to see another way, to see that her choice was the problem. Then she'd pretty much exploded the one thing that was good in her life in order to help her mother. Something she couldn't feel bad about, yet she knew, especially now, that there had been another way—if only she hadn't been quite so blockheaded about it all. But then, apparently being a blockhead was something she excelled at. With a groan she sat back down beside her mom. Janelle stared across the bed at the frail woman, watching her labored breathing.

One of the nurses came in a few minutes later. "I'm sorry that setting up the hospice care is proving to be such a hassle." She looked over at her mother. "Honestly, it's possible she may not make the trip."

"I know," Janelle responded. "I was hoping that she would just pass here, instead of putting her through that added stress."

"And she might. She might, indeed. If it's that close, they might not even move her because it's just harder on her."

Janelle didn't say anything to that, just nodded in agreement. Funny how the cancer specialist had told her that the flight home might do her mother some good at this point. Janelle was torn, not sure if yet another move would prove to be hard on her mother physically, or maybe it was more about how her mother wasn't necessarily here mentally anymore. Such a very strange situation for Janelle to find herself in, after the long battle with her mom's cancer, and it was not easy by any means.

When the nurse was gone, Janelle stared down at her phone, wondering at the sense of contacting Guilliam. Once again she reminded herself that she needed to give him space. However, after seeing him, she just wanted to be with him. She'd lost so much time with Guilliam, and she didn't have any decent understanding as to how their relationship had all gone to pieces—except that, back then, she'd felt Guilliam wasn't as understanding about her mother's condition as Janelle may have wanted. Still, looking back, she realized she had been acting out in more of a panic, and certainly not rationally.

Janelle hadn't realized how bad her mother's situation would get and what being her primary caregiver would require. Only experience gave her that information. So, at the beginning, she had been all in as far as caring for her mother. In the back of her mind she'd assumed that, when the cancer was gone, she and Guilliam could pick back up— if that's what they wanted. Three years ago, though, it hadn't even been a part of Janelle's thought process. So she'd more or less just bolted to her mother's side. And that was not without good reason. She had been very, very close to her mother growing up. Her mother had also adored Guilliam and had told Janelle that she was being a fool for breaking up with him, but she wouldn't listen.

Of course she wouldn't listen. That wasn't part of who she was, unfortunately. She seemed to spend more of her time making decisions that upset other people. She shook her head at that, realizing that no good would come from that speculation. Once she got this harsh memory out of her brain, it would be a whole lot easier.

As she sat there at her mother's bedside, Janelle checked her emails, checked in on work too. She was ever so grateful that she now had a work-at-home job where she could work part time and on her own schedule because it allowed her to keep busy while she was—and this was a terrible way to look at it—waiting for her mother to die. God, that made her feel so awful. She wasn't waiting for her mother to die. The reality was that her mother was dying, and it was a process, one that Janelle had never been through, a process she never wanted to experience, a process that left her struggling to do anything else that she needed to do.

It was horrific, plus incredibly sad and debilitating to watch. She hated to say it, but she was at the point where she could only hope that her mother would go to sleep one night and not wake up. Yet that's not what was happening. Instead it was this slow physical decline that also entailed a mental decline and was ten times worse than anything she'd ever thought it could be. There should be an easier way to check out when you got to this point in life. Why there wasn't one such exit, she didn't know.

If they could send people to all kinds of locations in the world, even to the moon, why wasn't there an easy way to make one's last days peaceful, kind, and gentle? Instead the physical body was ravaged, until it just gave out. Her mind resurrected one glimmer of hope from something she had read not that long ago. The theory was that our souls left our bodies before the final event, escaping some of the horrors that the family left behind had to deal with, if only vicariously.

She felt the tears choking up her throat again. She got up and walked over to the small bathroom, got herself a drink of water, and splashed some cold water on her face. When she heard a rattling noise, she walked over to the hospital bed and picked up her mother's hand. "It's all right, Mom," she whispered. "I'm here. It's okay."

Her mother opened her eyes briefly and sighed. "Yes, I know that you're still here. I just don't want to be here too."

Janelle winced because she didn't have any means to change the situation, and that hurt too. "Just go back to sleep," she whispered.

Her mother opened her eyes, looked up at her, and gave her a breathtaking smile. "I'll sleep, if you sleep too."

"I will. Honest."

Her mother shook her head. "Liar."

She winced because her mother always seemed to know. Janelle sat on the edge of the hospital bed and continued to hold her mother's hand.

Her mother whispered, "Don't be sad."

"I'm sad that you're suffering," Janelle clarified. And that was the truth.

Her mother gave her the gentlest of smiles. "Hopefully it won't be long now."

Janelle wanted to rail at her for being so complacent about it, yet who was she to say anything? Without even meaning to, she shared, "Guilliam's back in town."

Her mother slowly opened her eyes and stared at her. Miriam beamed with joy. "Good timing."

Janelle frowned at that. "What do you mean?"

"You'll need somebody when I'm gone," her mother whispered, "and it's always been him."

"But that doesn't mean he wants anything to do with

me," Janelle noted. "Remember how I'm the one who walked away from him."

"You were a fool," her mom replied. "I told you that."

The trouble was, her mother had, indeed, called Janelle a fool, but it wasn't exactly something she had been willing to hear back then. She watched as her mother's eyelids slowly closed again. Confirming that she was asleep, Janelle slowly returned to her chair.

Her stomach growled, and the thought of another hospital meal was enough to nearly break her. Plus, she didn't want to leave her mother and go down to the cafeteria either. Then she thought about Tesla, staying at her husband's bedside, constantly waiting, just in case he woke up, and realized that maybe she could do something for her friend.

Janelle quickly called Tesla and murmured, "I will head down to the cafeteria shortly. Do you want anything?"

"A juice would be lovely," Tesla replied in delight.

"How about tea?

"And tea would be lovely too," she agreed, her voice gentling at the thought. "How sad to think our world has come down to this right now."

"I know, and, while I'm so close to having this over, I still dread the fact that it will be over."

"Of course you do. You love your mom. The two of you were always very close."

"We still are. That's why I'm sitting here, waiting for her to fade away permanently. And I feel terrible because of that."

"That's because you love her, but you also don't want to see her suffer anymore."

"God no," she whispered back. "Look. I just … I need to get out for a few minutes. I'll pop down to the cafeteria.

What about food? Do you want a bite to eat?" she asked, returning to a more businesslike tone, so she wouldn't feel on the edge of tears.

"No, I think I'm fine for food," Tesla answered.

"You say that, but ..."

Tesla chuckled. "If they have any decent muffins, bring me one."

"Ah, *decent*, and that is where the problem lies, isn't it?"

"It is," Tesla agreed, with a groan. "But you never know, something *decent* could be there."

"I'll go take a look." And Janelle hopped up and ended the call. With another look at her mother, she headed to the cafeteria, several floors below.

She got in line, picked out a few muffins, grabbed a couple hot teas, one for Tesla and one for herself, and got the juice that Tesla wanted. As Janelle paid for them, she watched a man in a white coat casually walking through the cafeteria. She didn't think anything of it, but his hands were in his pockets, and he seemed deep in thought. *Just like any doctor*, she thought to herself. They dealt with people like her mom all the time. No joy in that job.

She wondered at the empathy and compassion so many of them possessed. It took a special person to work with the dying on a daily basis like this. She didn't think she could do it. She was dealing with dying on a daily basis with her mother, but it was hard, and not something she ever wanted to do again if she had such a choice. She wasn't sure if she did. This wasn't an easy pathway for her, and yet she was holding on, and that's what she would stick with.

She was holding on, and the rest of the world was holding on with her.

With a tray in hand, she turned and headed back up to

Tesla to drop off her goodies. She passed the doctor one more time as he leaned against a wall and stared out the windows at the end of the hallway. She smiled at him as she went by, then spoke to him. "You have a job I don't think I could ever do."

Startled, he stared at her.

She smiled as she added, "I'm finding it hard enough to deal with the slow death of a loved one. I can't imagine what it's like to deal with this on a daily basis."

He gave her a clipped nod and then shrugged. "You get used to it." And, with that, he turned and walked away.

Not exactly the answer she'd expected, but not everybody felt the same way about life and death as she did. Hell, she wasn't sure anybody did. She was as happy as anybody to live a good life, but, when the time frame of that good life ended, she wasn't sure there was such a thing as a good life anymore.

Yet so many people were out there who were such firm believers in heaven and hell, seemingly certain that people should be happy to go where they were intended. Janelle wondered if maybe she was the odd one out. Her mother hadn't been religious, with absolutely no belief in God or the devil. Her mom had done everything on her own as a single parent. She had been a huge blessing, and Janelle would miss her terribly.

Her mother's comment on Guilliam's *perfect timing* said much about her mom's worries about Janelle and how her daughter would manage when her mother was gone. As far as Janelle was concerned, she would grieve intensely for quite a while, and then, with any luck, she would gradually get over it, eventually moving on, holding the memory of her mother dear.

That was what she envisioned, though it wouldn't be easy to do. She couldn't imagine moving on as ever being easy. Her mother was such a special part of Janelle's world, yet hadn't been for a big chunk of her lifetime. Like so many children who grew into adulthood, Janelle had walked away, claiming her independence and carving out her own world on her own terms. Now she regretted so much of that, with absolutely no way to take it back, no time to go for a visit, to call her mom, to see how she was doing, or even to send her a message saying hi. The regrets were the part she would struggle with. With that, she checked in with the guard on Tesla's door, then walked in with the tray.

First, Janelle handed Tesla the tea. "Here you go," she said, with a smile.

Tesla looked up with a smile in return and reached out for the hot cup of tea joyously. "What is it about a cup of tea?" she murmured.

"Comfort," Janelle responded instantly. "It's all about comfort. And, boy, do we know what it's like to not have it."

Tesla nodded. "It's so hard, isn't it? You think you're doing well under the circumstances. You think that you've got this, and then it hits you sideways, and you realize you don't have it at all."

"But Mason, he's doing okay, isn't he?" she asked hesitantly.

"Yes. No. I guess," Tesla replied, with a small smile. "The doctors don't seem to be *unhappy* with his progress. What can I say? The head takes a long time to heal, apparently. I wasn't quite prepared for how long."

"Of course not," Janelle agreed. "I think that's the thing that nobody is ever prepared for. But, in the end, we'll all do just fine."

She chuckled. "We will, won't we? We will. How's your mom?"

"I hesitate to say that she's on her last days, but that's true. My mother is on her last days."

"And still no word on hospice?"

"No, I was just talking to a nurse, who suggested the possibility that she may not even make it to hospice."

Tesla winced at that. "God, I'm so sorry, … for all the good that does, I know."

"Better than anyone who doesn't think being sorry helps one bit. However, I so appreciate the empathy. So thank you for that."

Tesla nodded. "If there's anything I can do—"

"Look at you." Janelle burst out laughing. "The last thing you need to do is worry about me."

"I'm not worrying about you," she clarified, "but I'm concerned, and that's what friends are for."

"It is," she murmured. "I told Mom when she had a moment of lucidity that Guilliam was back."

"Wow. How did she react?"

Janelle snorted. "She said, *Good timing*, if you can believe that."

Tesla went oddly quiet for a moment. Then she started to chuckle. "I have to admit. I had the same thought myself,"

Janelle groaned. "That's not funny."

"It may not be funny, but it makes a lot of sense to me. You will need somebody."

"But he is far from *mine*, so he certainly won't be there for me at this stage of my life."

Just then some noise came from Mason. Tesla immediately got up to see to him.

Janelle waved. "I'll go, but let me know if there's anything else you need." And, with that, she sorted out the items on the tray and headed back to her mother's room.

Once again, as she walked down the hallway, she thought she saw the same doctor, the one from the cafeteria. This time he stepped out of what seemed to be a closet. It crossed her mind that maybe he was doing something inappropriate in the closet with somebody else. When he saw her, he frowned again. She just smiled and kept on walking.

If he was having an affair with somebody, Janelle couldn't quite imagine making out in a closet, not when anybody could walk inside. But what else did people do in closets? She shrugged, her mind not easily filling in that blank because nothing good would come of being in a closet or of potentially hiding there. She groaned, then turned and walked back. She called out to him, "Are you okay?"

He pivoted and frowned. "What are you talking about?"

The harshness in his tone surprised her, and she just shrugged. "Sorry. I just thought maybe you needed help." She walked away again. She didn't know why she'd thought he might need help. Hell, he was a doctor at this hospital, and, if anybody needed help, it was her. Still wondering at her rashness, she walked into her mother's room, realized that nothing had changed, then sat down once again ... to wait. To wait for the one or two golden moments when her mother would surface and would be lucid.

They were few and far between, but every one of them was something she treasured. Putting the rude doctor out of her mind, she settled into her vigil. Feeling an odd sensation, she turned and looked around, and the same doctor, poked his head in. He frowned. She frowned right back. "I don't think you're in the right room," she shared.

He glared at her, then snapped, "I don't think you're the

one to tell me that." He checked the room number, then turned and walked away, pulling out his phone and making a call.

She found herself wondering just what was going on. Something was incredibly suspicious about him, and yet maybe it was just her imagination. Maybe it was just a call about hospice. Hesitating, and now worried that she might have done something to mess up her mother's chances, she called out to him. He stiffened, then turned and glared at her. She winced. "Look. I'm sorry. We're trying to get my mother into the hospice. Is that what you're here about?" she asked hopefully.

He shook his head. "No."

Such a note of finality filled his tone that she had to wonder. Her shoulders sagged, and she nodded. "Okay, thanks anyway. However, if you do know how to help us, it would be appreciated."

He turned and glared at her again.

Frustrated, she threw up her hands. "Okay, sorry. I gather you're busy." She felt miffed at his attitude, yet did she have any reason to? Maybe it was because she was so damn short-tempered. Shaking her head, she headed back to sit with her mom. Still, something was off in his actions, something that she couldn't figure out.

Sighing, she sat back down again, determined to put him out of her mind. A little bit later she realized what was wrong. She recognized him, but he certainly hadn't been in doctor's whites back then. Not only that, he had been talking to the police. She reviewed that recalled information and would have to do something about it, even if not pertinent, if only to get it out of her brain.

She brought out her phone and asked Tesla to confirm

Guilliam's number. Seems it was the same one she had in her Contacts from three years earlier. She rewrote her text several times, and nothing she wrote made any sense. Finally she just phoned him. When he answered, his tone was surprised. "I know. I know," she admitted. "I probably shouldn't even be calling you, but—"

"But what?" he asked impatiently.

Most definitely a certain tone filled his words, but it was almost the same as the doctor, and that somehow managed to piss her off again. "It's probably nothing, and I get that, but I can't let it go."

"So, tell me then," he stated. "What is this *nothing*? Why can't you let go?"

"This man," she began, "the one who was just here, I don't think he's a doctor. I think he's here for some other reason."

Surprise filled his tone as he asked, "Okay, slow down. What are you talking about? Better start at the beginning."

"I don't know," she muttered. "Maybe I'm completely out to lunch."

"Maybe, and maybe not, but you need to tell me regardless. Now that you've started, you need to finish the conversation. What is it that's wrong?"

"The man," she repeated. "The last time I saw him, I think he was talking to a police officer."

"And?" he asked. "A lot of people get stopped and are asked questions. People see things, are involved in car accidents, all kinds of stuff."

"From the little bit that I overheard, it had to do with a gun, but I can't remember what it was about."

"I need more than that," he stated. "What do you mean about a gun?"

"I went to the station. It was a while ago, but he was there. He was helping a friend of his or something. It was confusing. Anyway, the two MPs were talking with him, but they let him go."

"And why were you there?"

"Because my car had been broken into, and I was hoping for some help."

"When was this?" he asked, his tone brisk.

"It must have been, I don't know. ... Maybe six months ago? I'm not sure."

"But you're sure it was him at the station."

"Oh, yeah, I'm sure it's him, no doubt. Yet I must admit, I've walked past him several times today, and it didn't register, not until he came to my mom's room."

"He came to your mother's room?" he asked.

"Yeah. And I talked to him, but just something is off, you know?"

"Yeah, I do know. Okay. Would you recognize him again in a picture?"

"Yes, of course. I just told you that I recognized him today. I was taking some photos earlier. I might have caught him in one of them."

"You may have taken a photo of him?" he asked.

"Yeah, I was taking a bunch of pictures. I get bored, just waiting. ... If I have a picture of him, I'll let you know."

"Yeah, look through your photos. I need to figure out who this guy is."

"I don't think he's very happy about the fact that I might have recognized him, but—"

"Did he know that you recognized him?" Guilliam asked.

"No, ... I guess not. Honestly, I don't know. I'm a mess,

so anything's possible."

After a moment of silence, he added, "Have a look at your phone and see if you've caught him in a photo. Did you say anything to upset him? Do I need to worry about him coming back after you?"

"Oh no, I don't think so," she replied. "Besides, he might just be having a bad day, and maybe he's truly a sweetheart."

"But you don't think so, do you?"

"No, of course I don't," she declared. "How could anybody so rude and curt be a sweetheart?"

"True," he murmured. "Anyway, go through your phone. Let me know if you find a picture of him. I can always get access to the hospital security cameras, but I'll need to have a reason."

"Right. I didn't think about that," she muttered.

"Where did you last see him?"

"He came by Mom's room, just a few minutes ago, but I did see him earlier on the same floor as Mason."

"What?" he asked.

"Yeah, I was bringing Tesla some tea. I didn't think about that though."

"Didn't think about what?"

Guilliam's exasperation shone through, pointing out how disjointed her conversation sounded. "I didn't think about what he was doing there. He was just leaning against a wall, maybe texting. And then I did see him again at a closet."

"Whoa, whoa, whoa, hang on a minute. You need to go back over this slowly. What exactly are we talking about here?"

"I don't know," she admitted. "I'm just telling you that I

saw this guy in a white coat, thinking he was a doctor, but he seemed suspicious. I'm pretty sure I've seen him before too, with that cop, but that's all I can tell you."

"Even that much is something," he noted. "So, repeat what you told me one more time." She went over it again, and he replied, "Okay. See if you've got a picture of him because I need to know who this guy is *now*, and we'll go from there."

"If you say so," she quipped, with a note of humor.

"Yeah, I say so," he snapped, his voice harsh.

She winced at that. "Look. I'm—I'm sorry. I didn't mean to upset you."

"It doesn't matter if you meant to upset me or not. Anything different, odd, or unusual that has to do with Mason's room is important. How's Tesla holding up?"

"Tesla is as she always is. Fine. That woman is a rock."

"She might be a rock, but she's also had a hell of a rough few weeks."

"I know. I didn't mean it in a negative way."

"I know you didn't. I just need to know more about this guy."

"It might be nothing."

"But, if you were suspicious enough to give me a call, then I will take it seriously."

"Fine. I'll spend the next little bit going through my photos to see if I can come up with an image."

"Right, and, if you see him again, don't do anything stupid."

She hesitated, then asked, "What does that mean?"

"It means, you leave him alone. Don't approach him. Don't start a conversation with him. If he talks to you, you just talk to him politely."

"Right. I did run after him because I thought he was a doctor and wondered if I'd messed up my chances to get my mother into hospice."

He repeated, "Hospice?"

"Yeah, she's—she's at the end but not quite," she explained. "I know it sounds terrible to put it that way."

"There's no good way to put it," he noted. "Anyway, send me those photos."

"Right. Will do," she muttered. And she ended the call and got to work searching her phone.

GUILLIAM GLARED AT his cell phone. They had just finished up at the airport, checking the angles on the sniper's shot at Mason. Nodding, not saying a word, he and Gideon were back in the car now.

At his side, Gideon asked, "Who was that?"

"An old friend. I haven't seen her in years, but she's in the hospital with her mother, who's apparently ready to go to the hospice." Then he gave his head a shake. "She saw somebody there today dressed like a doctor that she recognized from another time, like six months ago, when she saw the military police questioning the guy about a gun."

Gideon just nodded.

"And none of that would necessarily be an issue, but she says she saw him near Mason's room a little bit ago *today*."

"Okay, hang on a minute."

"I know. I know. She thinks she might have a photo of him and would certainly recognize him."

Gideon frowned. "We'll need to get those as soon as we can."

"We do. I was hoping that maybe … Could Jasper get some books over to her?"

"Maybe. I'm not sure exactly what we have to offer. I'll contact him, but I'm thinking it's probably all online instead of in physical mugs books. We'll put the guards on alert too."

"Right," Guilliam grumbled, kicking himself. "Everything's digital now, even mug shots."

"Only in some places," Gideon told him, with a smile, looking over at him as he parked at Drew's house. "Let's go," Gideon said, with a wave of his hand. "Let's make a quick trip inside. I already texted Jasper."

"If Jasper got the message from your short text," Guilliam stated, "he's better at communication than I thought."

Gideon laughed. "Jasper's very good at reading between the lines."

"He is, isn't he?" Guilliam glanced over at him. "You guys have known each other for a long time."

"We have. Worked together too for a while."

"Will you continue working with him?"

"Not sure yet. Why?"

"He mentioned a job, though I'm not sure I want one."

"Oh, you and me both," Gideon murmured. "I think he's looking at replacing all the former investigation staff."

"You mean, those two guys who were off to the side this morning?"

"Yeah."

"Why are they still there?"

"We're not sure," Gideon acknowledged. "Basically Jasper was told to bring in whoever the hell he wanted, so he did, and those original team members are not necessarily who he wants."

"Knowing Jasper, they're not even close to what he wants," Guilliam noted.

"Exactly. But you also know that he's not one to rock the boat until he has to. And, right now, he hasn't been able to clear any of those guys. So, until they've been thoroughly vetted, he doesn't want them operating with him. The original team lead, Morgan, was compromised and tried to kill Gideon and tried to sell the newest coroner to the highest bidder. So … we don't trust any of them. But this way, we keep the others close, so we can watch over them."

"Why the hell weren't they cleared?"

"That's a good question," Gideon stated, raising an eyebrow at him, "and we don't have an answer. A lot of their files are sketchy as hell, and you know how Jasper feels about that."

"Yep, I sure do," Guilliam confirmed. "Something that we'll have to give him a hand with, when this is over."

"Maybe. I think he's just hoping they'll all go away, though one of them already did—Steve, supposedly on medical leave."

"Are they upset about Mason getting shot?"

"I don't think they give a crap."

"In that case they need to go," Guilliam said, "because, if they aren't pissed off and fed up and upset, they don't belong here."

Gideon laughed. "That's exactly how I feel, but some of these guys seem more pissed off that Jasper's come in and stepped on their toes than about anything else."

"Boo-hoo," Guilliam replied. "I don't give a crap whose toes get stepped on, as long as the job gets done."

"That's why we're all here doing this job," Gideon stated, "because we all are friends and think the same way."

"No other way to think. A friend of ours, somebody decent, was shot down by a sniper on the goddamn base," Guilliam grumbled. "What's to think about?"

"I won't argue that," Gideon said, "because we're on the same page."

"It's just BS," he muttered. They walked into the small house, and Guilliam added, "From this one, I wanna go to the girlfriend's place."

They quickly did a walk-through of Drew's place. The forensics team was gone, so it wasn't an issue.

Guilliam frowned. "It's completely cleaned out."

Gideon sighed. "He gave up the lease and more or less just never showed up again."

"So, he had plans. As in *solid, in the works, we can do this* getaway plans."

"Yes, I would think so."

From there they went to the sniper's partner's place, a woman who called herself Suzan, now dead.

"And do we know for sure they were lovers?" Guilliam asked.

"It's possible. And it's also possible he ditched her because of the changes in his circumstances."

"And we don't know what that is either, do we?" Guilliam turned to face him.

"No, we sure don't," Gideon said. "There is a thought that they were in it together. There is also the thought that they were both more or less coerced into it. Still another thought is that they got in over their heads and would make a run for it. Yet another thought was he got paid and took the money and didn't want to share it with her."

"All of which are very good thoughts."

"Exactly. But these two people are dead, so we don't get to interrogate them and to determine just what they were thinking. We are pulling apart their lives for all known associates and family, but they kept to themselves pretty much. Now the woman's brother we *do* have in custody."

The second property, that of the girlfriend Suzan, didn't look viable either. He walked through the small apartment and shook his head. "She was leaving, wasn't she?" Guilliam asked.

"It looks that way, doesn't it?" Gideon came up behind him. "No bags or suitcases, so I presume she was staying someplace else, but she'd already left this place, if she was ever here long-term."

"And I'm not sure that she was," Guilliam muttered, with a nod. "It seems very much like either they were both running, or he was running without her."

"Which would have just pissed her off."

"Potentially, or what if she took something that she considered both of theirs, like the payday from doing a job?"

"And would that be both of theirs?" Gideon asked.

"I don't know. Maybe she was also pissed off because she knew what Drew had done and figured they wouldn't get out of it alive. I don't know. There are all kinds of scenarios that we'll have to take a closer look at. The bottom line is that they're both dead, and we didn't get to them in time."

"I'm not sure anybody could have got to them in time. They were targeted to die the minute they agreed to do the job."

Guilliam nodded. "That's what you and I would both do. If we had no intention of keeping our word, we would ensure that nobody got anything out of this deal."

"Unfortunately that's all too true in this case," Gideon

murmured. "And now we're only guessing at motives."

Guilliam took another walk through the place and frowned. "I had hoped there might be something personal here, and yet Suzan had already moved out—or had already arranged to meet with Drew somewhere else. Maybe she didn't know they had killed Drew. Maybe she thought Drew took off on her."

"Which also would make sense and would give her a good reason for being pissed off."

"Yet nobody mentioned anything about an attitude, about any hidden aggression on Suzan's part."

"Other than hitting Tristan on the head, nothing along that line came from Suzan, even when she asked questions of Drew's neighbor, Pearl, wanting to know if she was Drew's girlfriend," Gideon added. "So, I'm not sure that's quite the right track. Although, if Drew ditched her, she could be angry at him for that. Maybe Suzan was afraid that she would die next. Maybe she was hoping she could do something to keep them both alive."

"What about a safe deposit box or a locker someplace that may be tied to any of our suspects?"

Gideon frowned. "Could be one at the airport, but we would need the key, or we might find out something through security as to where everything is," he pointed out. "Then we might not need a key."

"It's possible, but I wouldn't worry about asking the authorities either," Guilliam cautioned, with a sideways glance at him.

"Agreed. We have to watch who we can trust, even here on base. Plus, we have this tangent case that was taken from us. I'm sure Jasper filled you in."

"Yep. Dirty officers high up in the military? Makes me

sick. Another reason not to ask anybody outside of our group."

"Good. We're all on the same page then."

"Right," Guilliam muttered. "Okay, back to a locker. What about a gym locker, a bus locker? What about—" Guilliam stopped. "If they were living off base, all kinds of options are there."

"I think they probably were, but is a gym locker the safest place to leave something incriminating?"

"Maybe not, yet what would they have done? If Suzan thought she and Drew were both in danger, what would she have done?"

"To keep them alive, if she had any blackmail material, she might have left that with a mutual third party," Gideon suggested, staring at him.

Guilliam frowned. "That could very well be what she's done. We just don't know who she would have left it with. Family?"

Gideon shook his head. "Drew didn't have any."

"What about Suzan's family?" Guilliam asked.

Gideon frowned. "A brother, in our lockup, who's very angry about her death."

"Still, if Suzan had regrets, wouldn't she leave these incriminating details with somebody like Mason, so he would know what happened? That way, maybe Suzan's killer gets taken out by Mason's men."

"But they must be pretty major regrets to do that," Gideon pointed out. "On the other hand, with people dropping like flies who are connected to this attempt to kill Mason, it's not out of the realm of possibility."

"Right," Guilliam agreed. "Still, we don't know enough yet, so we gotta keep our minds open."

They went back through her apartment, but it was essentially vacant, other than a couple big pieces of furniture. Guilliam walked over and sat down on the couch, shoving his hands in and around the couch cushions to confirm absolutely nothing was there. When he stood up, he rechecked the closet, looking on the shelves. "What about a purse? Did you find a purse?"

"Forensics has it."

"I think we need to take a look at that."

"If there was anything, they should have already found it."

"They should have, yes, but just like that special USB key, it might not be something easily visible or readily identified."

Gideon nodded. "We can go take a look."

"We may need Tristan to sweet-talk us into forensics. I understand he's become quite friendly with one of the ladies in the coroner's office."

Gideon nodded. "Yes, quite friendly with Amarylis, the newest coroner. She's also the one who recognized that USB key of Drew's for what it is."

"Ooh, I like it," Guilliam said, with a bright smile. "Smart too. I do like smart ladies."

Gideon gave Guilliam a wry smile. "So far, Jasper and the rest of us on his team have found our Keepers. I'm seeing the PT stationed on base. And hoping to become a whole lot friendlier on a more permanent basis." When Guilliam frowned, Gideon shrugged. "I know, not exactly what you expected to hear from me."

"No, but I trust your judgment. So, if this is it, this is it."

"And it is," he declared, with a huge smile. "I heard

there's a lady in town for you too."

Guilliam winced. "I don't know about *in town for me*." He had an odd expression on his face. "Let's just say that we have history."

"Lots of us have history," Gideon noted, "but this one of yours seems like maybe the history is ready to change."

"I don't know," he murmured. "Definitely not today's topic." And, with that, he willed it away. "Let's swing by forensics and have a look at Suzan's purse."

TESLA WOKE FROM another nap, stirred in place, and straightened to look around. She got up, walked over to the bathroom, and then called her family to confirm everything was okay. Her son, Sebastian, was with her father, and both were not allowed to come to the hospital again, as it had put targets on their backs. More volunteer guards were on them in rotating six-hour shifts as well. It pained her to be separated from her son, but thankfully her father kept the toddler busy. With a sigh, she told them both she loved them and ended the call.

She left the bathroom and returned to the hospital room to find Mason still sleeping, but at least it was a more relaxed sleep, and not that harsh, almost flat, nobody-at-home expression that he'd had earlier.

One of the nurses came in and smiled at her. "You're awake again."

"I seem to be sleeping most of my time away."

"Don't take that the wrong way," she murmured. "You're pregnant and under a lot of stress, so there are far worse things you could do for yourself than sleep."

"Maybe," she murmured. "And it is helping to make the time go by faster."

"Good, and he's doing much better."

"I think so," Tesla agreed, nodding, as she looked over at Mason. "It seems like there's a definite improvement in his breathing."

"And how are his cognitive functions?"

"He's been awake a couple times." She smiled broadly. "And he recognized me, so that's huge."

"Wow. Sounds like he'll do just fine in the end then. Just remember that the road to recovery will be stressful."

"And that's fine," Tesla noted, "as long as he recovers."

"We hear that all the time, from wives looking for that little bit of joy that says that their life will get back to normal."

"Of course it's what we all want," Tesla shared. "Every one of us just wants to know that our husbands will be back with us again."

"One of the nurses was given an envelope for you," she said, holding it out. "We didn't want to wake you. She did come by earlier, but you were out cold."

"Of course I was," she muttered. "Seems to be the standard state for me these days."

The nurse chuckled, as she handed it over.

"Why would somebody bring an envelope to the front for me?"

The nurse just shrugged. They talked another few minutes while the nurse checked on Mason, recording his vitals. Then she turned. "I'm leaving you now." And, with that, she was gone.

Tesla sat down with the envelope. Not recognizing the handwriting, she took a photo of it and sent it to Jasper.

He called her. "What is that?"

"I don't know. Someone left this letter with a nurse for me."

"Do you want me to come?"

"Is there any reason I shouldn't just open it?"

"Good question. How do you feel about it?"

"I don't understand why somebody would have left it."

Jasper groaned. "I'm on my way. Don't open it." And, with that, he hung up.

She stared down at her phone and winced. "I didn't mean to set off something new," she muttered. "For all I know it's nothing." But it could just as easily be something. This was her life now.

She sat back down and waited for her cousin to show up.

CHAPTER 2

J ANELLE GOT UP and walked to the doorway for what had
to be the twentieth time since she saw the doctor, or
whoever he was. And still saw no sign of anybody. She
hadn't found any photos, and that bothered her more than
anything. So now all she could think about was, if she caught
sight of him in the hallway, maybe she could take his picture.
She knew that Guilliam would have a heyday with her if she
did, but, in the absence of another photo, it made the most
sense to her. Maybe not to Guilliam, but she was used to
doing things that he didn't like. At this moment she was
much more concerned about finding out what the hell was
going on. Plus, this gave her something else to think about
besides her mother.

Her mother's hoarse breathing steadied in the background, yet Janelle knew that at any moment the hoarseness
could stop, and it could stop forever. She just couldn't bear
to even think about it. There had to be something else to
life. Yet here she was, struggling with the exact same questions she always had. Why was there always the threat of
death on such a permanent basis? Why hadn't we found a
way to make that stop yet? It sounded foolish to her, but
when you were faced with the loss of a loved one, she was

pretty sure that anybody would struggle to keep every moment they could.

Surely people were hungry for the opportunity to spend more time with those people they cared so much about. In their absence, it was important for the hospital staff to care for these people while they were here, to make their passing as easy as it could have been. Everybody died. No getting away from that. And Janelle wasn't afraid of death, but she sure wasn't a fan of all the multiple methods of getting there.

She considered whether she wanted to go for her umpteenth cup of tea and decided maybe not. Just enough was going on in her world right now that she was starting to feel a little bit like a teapot herself. She was pretty sure that Tesla didn't need any more drinks either. It was an activity, something to do, something different to think about. And yet, as Janelle sat there, with so many things still on her mind, so many thoughts running wild, she wasn't sure that the thoughts were even things she should be thinking about.

It just seemed as if so much in life didn't change for the good, how it was a constant litany of bad. She didn't want to think about it like that, but it was hard not to. The litany of bad was one thing, the constant issues something else altogether. It just felt like Janelle's last few years had been focused solely on her mom's health. Janelle had put everything else on hold so she could help her mom, and, now that the end was near, Janelle knew she would likely be conflicted, with a part of her feeling a sense of freedom, yet feeling a great loss.

Hearing footsteps, she looked down the hallway to see the same doctor again. He caught sight of her and glared. She had no idea why she'd set him off, and she was sorry because, if he'd done nothing or was completely innocent of whatever the hell was going on here, she would feel terrible. Yet it felt very much as if he was up to something.

If he was a doctor, great, fine. But if he wasn't, he shouldn't be impersonating one. And considering that Mason had been shot and nearly killed by some asshole, the last thing she wanted was anybody, good intentions or not, getting close to him. She watched as the suspicious man approached, thinking that he would change direction at the last minute, but he didn't. He just kept coming toward her. She stepped back into the hospital room, letting him pass.

She had her phone out, waiting to see if she would get the opportunity to get a picture of him. And yet how was she supposed to do that without letting him know? She didn't want to get in trouble, and she didn't want to piss him off either. If he had a right to be here, she would be the one in the wrong. Not that she particularly cared at the moment, since that seemed like the least of her worries. Yet maybe it was all wrong. When he walked past, deliberately ignoring her, she took a photo from the back, though it wouldn't be much help.

He turned around and asked, "Did you just take my picture?"

She frowned, noting that the shutter function did seem loud, even to her. "No. What are you talking about?"

He glared at her. "I don't take lightly to people taking my photo."

"Good to know," she said. "I'm standing here. You were walking past me. It's hardly a picture I would take. If you want me to take a picture of your front, your good side," she quipped in a mocking tone, "no problem."

He continued to glare at her. "I'll have you removed from this hospital if you do things like that."

She stared at him. "And yet I wonder if you even have any privileges in this hospital." He froze and she nodded. "I don't think you're a doctor at all—or even allowed to be here. So, the question is, why are you? What are you up to?"

He took a step toward her in a threatening manner, and she nodded. "See? That's what I mean. No way you're a doctor, certainly not when you go around uttering threats like that." He stiffened and glared at her. She shrugged. "I don't know what you're up to, but I bet it's no good."

"I don't know what you're talking about, but I will call security." And, with that, he turned and sauntered past.

She snorted and walked beside the stranger, deliberately took photos of him, almost in a mocking manner. She knew that Guilliam would be quite pissed at her, and so would Tesla for that matter, but it was something Janelle couldn't seem to stop herself from doing. This rude man had suddenly became a target for all the wrong things in her world right now. "You mean a picture like this? Or how about a picture like this?"

He tried to grab her phone, but she pulled it away. "Hell no. You get out of your stupid doctor's costume and get out of this hospital before you raise any more hell," she muttered. "Otherwise I will report you."

"You don't know anything."

"No, I sure don't, and I don't want to know anything, I just want you to stop harassing people."

"I'm not harassing people. You are."

She snorted. "Nice try. That won't work."

"Sure, it will because you don't know what the hell you're talking about."

"Maybe not, but I don't think you do either. And this place probably frowns on people like you, dressing up like doctors when they're not doctors at all."

He cried out, "I am a doctor."

And this time just enough frustration filled his tone to make her pause. "But are you? Are you really?"

"Yes. What the devil would make you think I not?"

She frowned. "Your mannerisms." He just stared at her, and she nodded. "It's as if you're *acting*."

"And that is BS." He brushed her aside and snapped, "Get lost, and get out of my life. I have patients to look after."

"Yeah, *patients*," she repeated in a loud tone. "But are you a medical doctor trained to look after these patients, or are you just a piece of shit out there causing chaos?"

He stopped. "You're crazy, right? I don't know what your problem is, but obviously whatever is going on in that room has affected you. And obviously you're not handling life very well." She glared at him, and he continued. "You're seeing boogeymen when there aren't any. So maybe we should get you some help. I can arrange that," he declared, with a brilliant smile in her direction.

She felt a creepy coldness on the inside at his words. "Oh, I don't think so," she replied softly, "but thanks so much for the offer."

And with that, he turned and walked away, and she slowly returned to her mother's room. She probably should not have antagonized him that way, and, for the life of her, she didn't even realize why she'd done it. It just seemed like something she needed to do. She had to find out if something was wrong. It was as if she'd been inactive with such a singular focus for so long that this was the first thing she could jump at and could make a difference, make some sense of things. Yet what she'd done had been the antithesis of common sense.

She groaned as she sat back down, sending the photos to Jasper in a text, knowing there would likely be repercussions for her actions. She just wasn't sure who she would hear from yet, but she knew it would be coming and just sat down to wait.

GUILLIAM STOPPED, STARED down at the text in his hand, frowned, then called Jasper. "What was that about?" he asked.

Jasper gave a bark of laughter. "Don't ever tell me that she doesn't matter."

"I won't say that she doesn't matter," he clarified. "Now, what do you mean she challenged the impostor?"

"Yeah. He came by, and she decided she wanted a photo of him because she didn't have one, so she approached him and got one."

"Good God, that could be dangerous."

"She said it was an impulse that she couldn't resist, doesn't have a clue why, and put it down to a life of sheer boredom at the moment and needing something meaningful to do."

"Christ," he muttered, pushing his hair back. He'd meant to get a haircut before coming in. His hair was a little longer than he liked and longer than most people would be accustomed to seeing him with. Plus, it had the habit of getting in his way all the time now. "I'm going to the hospital. We're just about done here."

"Good enough," Jasper noted. "I'm giving you access to the online mug shots. So when you stop in, talk to her yourself as she goes through the photos."

"Have you talked to her?" he asked in alarm. "Is she in any danger there?"

"I don't think so, but I don't know for sure. I did talk to her, and I've got the photo that she sent me. It's not great, but it is something. I'm hoping, if we give her access to the mug shots, she'll pinpoint a better one."

"Good enough. I'm heading to the hospital. Send me the link, and I'll bring it up on my laptop."

"Okay. She's got a laptop there too."

"Good. I'll be at the hospital pretty quick." And, with that, he hung up and looked over at Gideon. "Can you drop me off at the hospital?"

"I can," Gideon agreed with a nod, as they headed back to the car. "What's the matter?"

"Remember the lovely lady who everybody is so sure is in my life?"

"Yeah. What about her?" Guilliam explained what she'd done. Gideon frowned. "This is the guy who was lingering on the same floor as Mason?"

"Yes."

"Anybody ask the guard there about him?"

"I don't know, but I will when I get there. I was hoping to get a photo of this guy so we can see if he's hanging around on a regular basis or if it was just the one time. Because, for all we know, he is a doctor on staff who just lost a patient and needed a moment or something."

"Right. Is she paranoid?"

"Not normally, but I haven't had much to do with her in the last few years," he pointed out.

"Right. Of course. It's always hard to figure out who a person is after you've missed a significant time period with them, isn't it?"

"It is. I wasn't expecting to deal with her on this trip."

"The minute you're not expecting to deal with somebody," Gideon noted, "that's when they show up, and it's something you definitely must deal with."

"Maybe. It's not what I thought I would be doing today."

He chuckled. "I don't think anybody thought you would be doing this today."

"Good point," he muttered. As they headed to the hospital, Guilliam shook his head. "I can't believe she got into an altercation with him. Now he's bound to remember her for sure."

"Do you think it's serious?"

"Knowing her? Yeah."

"Didn't I ask you if she was the kind to get into trouble?"

"You did. And I would have said no, but a few other things are popping up in my brain."

"And what did she say about going to the cops?"

"Something about her vehicle being broken into," he shared.

"Do you think it's connected?"

"I don't know why it would be, especially when it was maybe six months ago," he noted, as he looked over at Gideon. "But thanks for that thought."

Gideon shrugged. "Right now, it seems that everything is potentially connected—anything and everything. We have to unravel it all before we find out how to disconnect it."

Guilliam didn't say anything to that, but he knew Gideon was correct. Guilliam tried hard not to deal with these shittier things in life. He honestly didn't want to deal with her. Particularly not right now, not when his emotions were still raw and when he hadn't had any time to sort out how he felt about her. "It sucks. I wasn't thinking this would be on my plate when I came back to help."

"And yet maybe it's a good thing," Gideon suggested, looking over at him.

"How do you figure that?"

"She's clearly on your mind. She's here, and she's dealing with trauma of her own, and whatever it was that you guys had between you before, it might be time to find some closure, one way or another. If it's a no-go, then obviously you write her off. And, if it *isn't* a no-go, then maybe it's time to decide just what you guys may have."

"Did I say it was a go?"

"No, you sure didn't," Gideon confirmed, "but the fact that she's causing you trouble means you haven't dealt with it." He stared at him and then smiled. "You're welcome."

Guilliam groaned. "I don't like it when my personal life becomes my public life."

"Nobody does," he pointed out. "Absolutely nobody does. But that doesn't change the reality of what's in front of you right now." And, with that, he pulled into the hospital parking lot and stopped at the main entrance. "Good luck."

"Great," Guilliam muttered, as he hopped out. He took one look around and added, "I should have just driven on my own."

"No need. If you need wheels, let me know. I'll come get you, or I can arrange for your car to be brought over."

"Just arrange for my car to be brought over, will you?" he asked handing over his keys. "That would help a lot."

"Good enough. Good luck."

With his laptop and his duffle bag in hand, he quickly

headed into the hospital. As he got closer to Janelle, he stopped, preferring to detour to say hi to Tesla for a moment. While he was there, he spoke to the guard. As soon as he mentioned the suspicious doctor to the guard, the guard nodded.

"Yeah, he was here earlier today," he muttered. "Looked as if he'd had one of those days. We all get those days. He was just leaning back with his eyes closed, half muttering to himself. I didn't know if he was talking himself into doing something or talking himself out of it," he shared, with a laugh. "He seemed harmless enough."

"Good enough. However, if he comes back, I want you to keep note and to let me know immediately."

"Sure enough. Do you think he's a problem?"

"I don't know who's a problem and who's not at this point," Guilliam admitted. "Let's just make sure that we don't make any assumptions." And, with that, he popped in to see Tesla, surprised to find Jasper sitting beside her. They were looking at an envelope.

Jasper looked up, frowned, and explained, "Yeah, Tesla had an envelope delivered today."

"What's in it?"

A note was in a plastic evidence bag, and Jasper passed it over to Guilliam.

He read it out loud. "*I'm sorry. If I could have had it go another way, I would have.*" Guilliam stared at it. "Ah, hell. Do we think this is from the shooter? Arranged before his death?"

"I think it's definitely from somebody *connected* to the shooter," Jasper noted. "I'm also thinking that it might be from our female who didn't make it—Suzan, supposedly a girlfriend to Drew, the sniper."

Guilliam pondered that as he looked at the note.

"And yet it doesn't give any other information."

"No. And that's a bit of a trigger for me too. If you turn it over, you'll see a series of numbers and the word passports." Then he pointed to where they were written on the back of the envelope itself in tiny letters.

"Oh, now that's suspicious in itself."

"But is it suspicious, or is it enlightening?" Tesla asked, staring at him.

Guilliam grinned. "In this case, it's probably a hell of a good thing. I'm not sure what those numbers mean, but it looks to be"—he glanced at Jasper—"a safe deposit box or a personal wall safe or something along that line."

"I agree with you," Jasper replied. "I've taken a photo of the numbers, and forensics is on it. It just means that this lady of secrets, or whoever wrote this note, had a few more that we have yet to expose … or just an exit planned, which would make more sense," Jasper warned.

"In which case I like Drew for that. He'd had to have had an exit plan when he didn't want to kill Mason. So that's going to be where he stashed his, and possibly Suzan's passports. Not sure we'll ever find it though."

The two sat in silence considering actions of people no longer around.

"I'm heading over to Janelle's mother's room," Guilliam announced. "I'll get her to go over the mug shots to find our suspicious doctor. According to the guard, somebody fitting Janelle's description of the strange man was outside Mason's room today. The guard didn't see him as a threat, but I told him that we will treat it as a threat until further notice."

"Of course," Jasper agreed. "I asked him if anything seemed to be suspicious, but he said no."

"That's because he didn't think this guy was anything to worry about. I'm just telling you that I don't think we can mark him off as *not* being suspicious. At least not until we figure out who he is."

"No, of course not," Jasper muttered. "I'll talk to the guard myself, when I leave. We'll need to keep on top of that at each shift change as well."

With a quick nod to Jasper and a hug for Tesla, Guilliam turned and headed out to meet with Janelle.

CHAPTER 3

JANELLE LOOKED UP when she heard a voice come from the door. Surprised, she hopped to her feet and walked over to Guilliam. "Hi," she greeted him, a smile in her tone as she studied his face. "You look tired."

He nodded as he searched her face. "Are you okay?" he asked, his voice gentle.

She nodded, then shrugged. "I'm okay. Tough times here though."

"I know." He turned to face her mother in the hospital bed and sighed. "It's hard to see her like this. She was so full of life. So, nothing that they could do to treat this, *huh*?"

"No. She fought and fought hard, until, one day, no more fight was left in her," Janelle shared. "And then Mom asked to stop the treatments."

He winced. "And you let her?"

"Ah, you know me so well," she muttered, a note of bitterness in her tone. "I fought her on it, but she was tired, and she was ready to go."

"Your father has been gone for many years."

"Yes. I'm sure that played a part in her decision too—not to mention the fact that the doctors kept telling her they could keep trying, but they didn't hold out any hope."

"Well then, if there's no hope, it makes you question what you are putting her through and why."

"Exactly, and that was the point I came to," she murmured. "It wasn't easy, but we're here now. And it will all be over soon."

"When you say *soon*, what does that look like?"

She shrugged. "They're looking for a hospice placement, so I would say less than a month, maybe less than a couple weeks. Today one of the nurses told me that Mom may not make it to hospice and may go while she's here."

He nodded, then walked over to stroke her mother's hand. "I always loved her."

Janelle felt tears in the back of the throat at that. "I'm sure you won't appreciate this, but, when I told her this morning that you were back, the first thing she said was, *Good timing.*"

He asked, "Why would she say that?"

"Because she's worried about me," she replied, "as are a lot of my friends."

"Of course. This has been your life for a long time, hasn't it?"

She nodded. "Yes. A very long time," she murmured, as she stared down at her mother. "While it's been an honor and a joy, it's also been damn hard, the hardest thing I could ever do."

"I'm sorry. I didn't understand what it would do to you."

"How could you? Honestly, I had no idea what I was in for," she explained. "So, why would you know? How can anybody understand the process, particularly when you expect that it will turn out fine, only to then suddenly find out it's not fine at all? You're just dealing with the aftermath and the slow decline." She shrugged. "It's been one of the hardest battles I've ever had to face. And it wasn't even mine."

"It was definitely yours," he corrected, as he walked to her. "It was your battle because you are here for her, come thick or thin. You should be proud of the battle you waged, and she needs to be at peace with the battle she waged. And, if she's ready to go, and it's her time, then she'll go," he stated. "No guilt. No wish-we-could-haves," he murmured. "It's all about one day at a time and getting through this next stage of your life."

She sniffled several times and let out a long breath, not sure what to say. In a way, it was wonderful to hear him speak this way and lovely to have this conversation, mostly because part of her still felt guilty that she couldn't get her mother to fight anymore. However, there just wasn't anything more that could be done to save her mom. Janelle understood, yet she didn't understand at all. Who could understand it? It was all too much. Too much pain, too much torment, and too difficult to watch somebody you loved and cared for so deeply go through this.

As she reached for the Kleenex in her bag one more time, he sat down beside her. "I have access to the criminal database, so I was hoping you could take a look and see if you recognize anyone."

She nodded and pulled out her phone. "Don't bother yelling at me. This is all I have." Then she held up the picture on her phone.

He looked at it and frowned. "*Ha.*"

"What's *ha?*"

He went back to his laptop, brought up the site that he was looking for, then flipped through it, finding something.

It quickly became obvious that he was looking for something specific.

Janelle realized that maybe Guilliam recognized the fake doctor too. She waited and waited, until suddenly he brought up an image.

"Him?" he asked.

She looked at it and then slowly nodded. "Yes, him. How did you know?"

"Just something about that tilt of his chin. I've seen him before. As a matter fact, I think we've …" He frowned. "As much as I don't want to say it this way, I think we've been up against him before."

She stared. "What does that mean?"

"Nothing good. Absolutely nothing good. So, you're sure this is him?"

She nodded. "Yes, it's absolutely him."

"I need a moment." Then he got up and went out into the hallway to make a phone call.

She didn't need to be within earshot to know that he was upset, and obviously it revolved around this man. She studied the photo on the laptop. His name was Scott Smith, which sounded like an alias to her. He supposedly had the nickname of Scotch. She didn't know how he got such a nickname, but still the man in question didn't speak with an accent or anything. She studied his face for a long moment and realized the mug shot was a good likeness. If he appeared to be slightly older now, that would be normal, even expected.

Then Guilliam came back and sat down beside her.

"Are you going to get him?" she asked.

"We'll certainly start hunting for him. How long ago did you see him here?"

She thought about it and winced. "It's probably been just over an hour."

He nodded. "We will get access to the hospital camera footage and see where all he went."

"I'm sure the hospital will love that."

"They had somebody impersonating a doctor on their premises," he pointed out. "Believe me that anything I do is nothing compared to what the media would do if they find out."

"I mentioned that to him."

He stopped and stared at her.

"I know. I probably shouldn't have mentioned anything."

"You shouldn't have spoken to him at all about anything," he stated. "The fact that you did blows me away."

"It blows me away too," she muttered. "I just wanted to get a picture of him, so I could send it to you, to see whether this was a problem or not. And then he comes by, caught me taking a picture and got angry."

"Not to mention the fact that it might break a few laws. You're generally not allowed to photograph people if they don't want to be photographed."

"It's not as if he's allowed to impersonate a doctor either," she argued caustically.

"So, how did you know he wasn't a doctor?"

"He was just roaming the hallways, looking a bit on the lost side," she began. "It just seemed wrong. Doctors are here, but they're busy. They come and they go, but they do it with intention. They're never just wandering around lost in the hallways."

He nodded. "I can see how that would get your attention."

"I'm here all the time," she noted. "I don't pop out of Mom's room all the time, so I definitely don't get to see my fill of doctors. In my situation, I'm always waiting, hoping to speak to a doctor. And, when you do, they come and go quickly. You get to know their routine to the degree that you can, specialists aside, so you can speak to them. This guy just didn't check any of those boxes."

"Okay, good enough." Guilliam smiled. "You're right. He isn't necessarily somebody you would have recognized in a white coat, except that he was acting *off*, which caused you to look at him more closely."

"Exactly," she agreed. "And I saw him enough times in that same *lost* state that it bothered me. Then I started making a point to pay closer attention and to watch for him."

He pondered that. "You mentioned how you saw him come out of a closet."

"Yes. And I didn't have the best thoughts right off the bat. I was thinking, oh great, that doctor probably had some sweet young nurse in there, and they were banging it on the counter." His eyes widened at her phrase. She shrugged. "It wasn't exactly a flattering first thought."

"No, it doesn't sound like it," he agreed, his lips twitching.

She glared at him. "There's always shit going on in a place like this, but you just don't really see it."

"And nobody wants to see it either," he pointed out.

"No, and that's part of the problem. It seemed to me like he shouldn't have been in the closet. I guess that's what I wanted to say, and I didn't know why he was there."

"Probably getting his doctor's coat," Guilliam suggested.

She stared at him and murmured, "I didn't even think of

that."

"Who knows what he was really doing, and that's not an issue for you," he replied, "but I don't want you aggravating him."

She snorted. "You mean, aggravate him any more than I already have?"

"You may have chased him away, and that'll make it that much harder for us to find him."

She winced. "Ah, jeez, I didn't think of that either."

He smiled. "It's not the end of the world if you did. We'll find him. I promise."

"Sure," she muttered, "but it still makes me feel shitty."

He winced. "That's not my intention, and I don't want you feeling shitty. I just want you to look after yourself, so it's not a horrific deal that blows back on you."

She nodded. "I can do that."

He hesitated, then added, "I'm not even sure it's safe to leave you here."

She looked at him in surprise. "Why? Because of the altercation I got into with our fake doctor?"

"Yeah," he said. "Think about it. This guy potentially could make your life very difficult."

"He's not a doctor, so, if he's trying to get me kicked out, as he threatened he would, that will only cause troubles for him," she muttered.

"I don't think he's worried about kicking you out," Guilliam replied. "More to the point is that he would have picked up on the idea that you could now recognize him, and, after the altercation, you may very well have told somebody."

"And you think that will cause me some trouble?"

He looked over at her and asked, "What do you think?"

She winced. "I don't know what to think because I don't know who this guy is or what he's up to. I just think it's a shitty deal that he gets to walk around like that."

"Sure, but the fact that he's been doing that also means that he's up to no good, and, if he's up to no good, what lengths will he go to in order to keep you from telling anybody that you saw him, and that you saw what he was doing?"

She stared at him. "So now, what you're telling me is that I could be in danger."

He groaned, then sat back. "Yes. I believe you could be in danger." She glared at him, and he shrugged. "What do you want me to say?"

"There's nothing to say," she noted. "I don't normally get into trouble, you know."

"Normally?" he repeated. "I can recall a couple times where you got pretty upset."

"Sure, but that was over injustices," she muttered. "It's not fair for you to bring that up."

He laughed. "It might not be fair," he pointed out, "but for bad guys up to no good, I don't think *fair* will be very high on their list of issues."

"So, what do I do then?" she asked. "I can stay out of his way."

"But he knows what room you're in, right?"

"Sure, but I'm not leaving my mother," she declared, her voice adamant. "No way. I'm here right through to the bitter end."

"I get that," he said, "and I understand that. It would be awfully nice, though, if we had a way to keep you from getting into any more trouble."

"How do you propose doing that? Even if they move us,

the fake doc will still be around, so he'll still hassle me if he sees me. And, if he wanted to find me, if he's got any skills at all, he could certainly do so."

"Maybe, and it could be a whole lot more than hassling you," he pointed out. "That mug shot name is fake as well. So we don't know who this guy is or what he is up to, and I don't want him coming back to stop you from saying anything to anybody."

She sat back and glared at him.

He nodded. "I know. It's not what you want either. However, you pulled the tiger's tail, and that tiger, in theory, could be very dangerous."

She stared off into the distance. "That would really suck if somebody's out there, making my life even more difficult."

"Yeah, well, I'm guessing he is probably out there somewhere, thinking *you*'re the one making his life difficult."

She nodded, followed by a chuckle. "You're right. I think he probably is." She groaned. "What have I gotten myself into this time?"

"I don't know, but I sure wish you weren't in the middle of it."

She looked over at him and nodded. "Again, I didn't do it on purpose."

"Maybe not, yet here you are," he said. "And it's not something we can get you out of that quickly."

"I'm staying right here too," she repeated, as she looked around the room. "So, I'm not sure there's anything we can work out to change the situation."

"We have to come up with a working solution," he replied. "I just don't know what it will be. I'll talk to the others, and we'll sort it out. In the meantime, if you see him at all, you tell me immediately. If you do see him, please don't approach him, don't say anything to him, don't do anything."

She glared at him but nodded.

"And, yes, I'm serious. We don't know what he's up to. But, if he's somehow involved in the attack on Mason or these associated issues, for all we know, you could be his next victim."

GUILLIAM SIGHED. FRUSTRATED that Janelle didn't seem to be getting the message, he arranged with the hospital to relocate her mother and requested a private room at his expense. He wasn't sure if the insurance money would cover it or not, but the hospital was okay to move her, so long as somebody would pay for the additional costs. When Jasper contacted him a little later, he explained what he had done.

"That's a start," Jasper noted, "but it's not likely to be a final solution."

"I know. It's frustrating because we have no way of knowing when he might find her again. I keep hoping that something will break first."

"Oh, I think something is bound to break," Jasper stated. "We've got some new information at least, and one of the guys we have in custody has decided to talk."

"Good. Now if we can find this asshole at the hospital, pretending to be a doctor, I will take that as another big sign."

"You think he's connected?"

"I wouldn't if he hadn't showed up near Mason's room too. That, and his other actions are suspicious enough that we have to consider it a real possibility and take more precautions."

"I agree with that," he murmured, "and I've told Tesla, so she's on the lookout."

"That's good, though it might not be enough to change anything."

"Might not be, but that's not the point. What's important is that everybody is aware. Did we deal with intel sharing for shift changes of the guards?"

"Yes, and we put two extra guards on, starting today, just because of it."

"Good," Jasper muttered. "I wish our fake doctor would take a chance and would try to get to somebody. At least then we could stop his attempt and have another guy to interrogate. The one guy in jail who's interested in talking wants a free pass."

"That ain't happening," Guilliam snapped, anger curling through his tone as he thought about the crime against Mason that had started all this.

"I know. And you can bet that none of the bosses are too inclined to give in to him either, but they also know that we need to solve this thing, and need to do it quickly. It's been too long already."

"I know," he conceded, "which is why I'm here now."

"And that's great and proving to be helpful already. I mean, you've got a girlfriend in the hospital who has, right or wrong, identified a shady character."

"But he's also on our list of majorly shady characters," he pointed out.

"Yes, you're right in that sense, so we need to find him, but now I want you to come talk to our prisoners."

"Oh, I would love to have a crack at them," Guilliam replied, "particularly in the mood I'm in."

Jasper snorted. "Not sure anybody would be okay with you beating the crap out of them," he noted, "but I'm more than willing to step out and turn a blind eye."

Guilliam laughed. "Generally that's not required, and my sunny disposition does the trick, but I'll hunt you up when I get done."

"You do that," Jasper said, with a chuckle.

Taking his leave of the hospital, glad that Gideon had someone drop his car off, Guilliam headed down to the investigators' office and to the holding area where the three men were being kept. Two were in a cell together, and one of those two wanted a deal.

As Guilliam walked in, the guy crossed his arms and stared at him with a bored expression. Guilliam just shrugged, turned, and walked right back out again.

"Hey, wait," the guy called out.

Guilliam stopped at the doorway, pivoting to face him. "Wait for what?" he asked. "I've got no time to wait."

"No, I get it. I hear Mason's still alive though."

"He is, and that just means some asshole is likely to make another attempt."

The prisoner immediately nodded. "Yes, and I think that is exactly what will happen."

"We already have somebody at the hospital acting suspiciously."

His gaze widened at that news.

Guilliam nodded. "He's not very good at whatever he's supposed to be doing."

The other guy winced. "Right, sometimes you can't get good help," he muttered.

"Maybe, but, in a case like this, it's definitely to our benefit that idiots are out there, hiring more idiots."

He shrugged. "Not my deal."

"*Not your deal* won't be your deal because you're heading to prison," Guilliam stated. "So I don't give a shit what you want." The prisoner just glared at him, and Guilliam shrugged. "If you've got something to say, say it. Otherwise I've got another prisoner to talk to."

"I already said what I wanted."

"Yeah, that's nice and not happening. You're headed for life in prison, and honestly, I don't give a damn if they throw away the key. You're also looking at being court-martialed. So, as far as I'm concerned, that will be way worse than anything the civil system will give you."

The other man didn't say a word.

Guilliam turned to walk out.

The prisoner called out again, "Hang on."

Bored, Guilliam turned. "You've got two minutes to give me a reason not to walk out."

"Oh, I have a good reason. That suspicious guy in the hospital? He's not really good at his job, but somehow he always manages to get the job done."

"He's looking for Mason, I presume."

The other guy nodded. "He's just another one of the lackeys."

"We're already looking for him, and Mason's got triple guards, so the chances of somebody getting through to him are not great. We're doing everything we can to ensure that nobody gets a second chance at him. Right now we're more interested in finding out who put this in motion and why."

"I don't know about the why," the prisoner replied. "All I know is that it had to do with somebody Mason killed."

Guilliam frowned. "Mason's job required him to kill dozens."

"I know," the guy said, with a nod. "Maybe you should be looking at the people in question."

"We already are, but, so far, nothing in particular has popped."

He shrugged. "That's because you're thinking missions. You need to be thinking closer to home." And, with that, he shut up, but added, "That's all I'm giving you."

Guilliam walked out of the temporary holding cell section into the main building for the investigative team. He found Masters and Jasper standing there, waiting on him.

"What did he say?" When Guilliam told them, Jasper stared at him and repeated, "*Closer to home and not a mission. We have flagged several cases that fit that bill, where Mason's been involved in it*," he murmured.

"How bad were they?"

"Some were bad. Some might even have involved Tesla," he noted.

"When you say, *involved Tesla*, what does that mean?"

"One was a home invasion of a friend of theirs. After the home invasion, the friend got pissed off when he found out that nobody was interested in following up on it. Mason started to apply pressure for an investigation. It wasn't handled within the military, so the local cops were dealing with it. However, there wasn't a whole lot of evidence, so the case remains active. Then somebody came after Mason and attacked Tesla."

Guilliam's eyebrows shot up. "I didn't hear about that."

"Right, because Mason dealt with it the way Mason always deals with stuff, cold and efficient. The guy died on the spot. It was a clean kill because the guy was in Mason's house, holding a gun to Tesla, clearly after revenge. It was the same guy from the home invasion of Mason's friend."

"So, what then? A family member coming for justice? Do we have some punk out there who's related to this dead intruder, who decides Mason's to blame? This sniper shooting of Mason is one huge op for some Joe Blow to fund."

Jasper nodded. "If you consider that this guy went after Mason because Mason was trying to solve the case for this friend of theirs, it makes sense that maybe our mastermind comes from the same gene pool."

"So, in other words, friends or family."

"Exactly. And that would also explain why none of these names or cases are in our files."

"Agreed. Which means we need to go to town and talk to the local police."

At that, Jasper grinned. "I know exactly who you need to talk to."

"Good. Give me the details, and I'll be on my way."

It took about thirty-five minutes to get to the police station, and, when he walked in and asked to see Chief Princeton, he was surprised to see a woman waiting for him.

She smiled. "I see Jasper didn't give you a heads-up. I'm Alex Carlon-Princeton, Chief of Police."

He shrugged, reaching out to shake her hand. "He spoke highly of your work in the position. If you have information you can help us with, I would appreciate it."

"I pulled up the file that Jasper mentioned, when he called earlier today. How is Mason doing?" she asked, looking over at him.

"As well as he can at this point. He's alive and has surfaced a couple times, then goes right back under. But that's not necessarily a bad thing because, if he wakes up, and we haven't got this solved, we are not keeping that man in the hospital."

Her face cracked with a beaming smile, as she nodded. "You've got that right. So, I didn't realize we were looking outside of his military career."

"We are again looking at Mason's own home invasion."

Her face sobered up immediately, and she nodded. "Yes, but it was a clean kill. Somebody came in with the intent to hurt them."

"I get it. A man has a right to defend his own home, to protect his family. Believe me that I understand. I'm not blaming Mason in any way, but Mason killed an intruder. Whether legally or not, that doesn't mean that somebody close to this dead intruder might have a different idea of justice."

"No doubt the kid who stupidly broke into Mason's home—and his friend's house earlier—was doing it more for a lark and because he was bored."

Guilliam sat back and stared at her. "The kid was bored? The one involved in the home invasion?"

She nodded. "He had a very entitled lifestyle, and he didn't have enough eyes on him to keep him out of trouble, apparently. As far as he was concerned, life was just—"

"Names?" he said quickly.

She handed him a piece of paper. "I already summarized what information there was on both home invasions, plus a list of the dead intruder's family and friends. It's not a whole lot of names."

"But it confirms that this is the guy who was doing the home invasions."

She nodded. "Yeah, and apparently he bragged a fair bit to Mason, while he was in their home, holding a gun to Tesla's head."

Guilliam winced at that. "That's a death sentence right there."

She nodded. "I hear you, and I get it, but we still can't have any vigilante justice."

"So, it is correct to assume that the parents of this kid had an issue with what happened?"

"They called it murder, and of course it wasn't, but they also didn't want to believe that their son had been involved in all these B&Es. Of course they miraculously all stopped once he was dead. Plus, he confessed to Mason, who had it recorded. Still, the parents claimed it was under duress, even though he was clearly bragging about it."

"Right. So, we have a typical father, who doesn't want to believe his kid's a bad seed."

"Typical well-to-do father who believed his kid could do no wrong," she added. "That's always a problem."

"Definitely a problem," he muttered. "Not fun."

"No, not for any of us," she replied. "I took quite a bit of flak over it all. The locals were fine with it, of course, because all the break-ins stopped. Plus, the son had started to go over the edge a little bit."

"Meaning?"

"The kid took trophies from the houses he broke into. Underwear—ladies' underwear, of course."

"Aw, shit," Guilliam muttered. "This guy was on his way to becoming a rapist then, and that probably would have progressed pretty quickly."

"He did threaten to rape Tesla, right in front of Mason," she shared.

Guilliam stared at her in shock, and she nodded. "Wow," Guilliam replied. "Did the kid know who she was?"

"I don't know. Mason was upset for this friend, who had

been the victim in a prior B&E. Mason came to me about his friend's home invasion, which was already on my docket, but we just didn't have any evidence of who was involved. Mason pretty well set himself up as bait, publicly promising to take down this guy, suggesting that his place be next on the list."

"Ah, crap, such a Mason thing to do. I am surprised he did it with Tesla there though."

"She wasn't supposed to be there. She was going to her father's, but then something came up at work, so she returned home, which put her right in the line of fire. Mason had no idea she was there. So, when he came home, he found her with this guy. It didn't take long for things to escalate."

"No, it wouldn't. Jeez, poor Tesla. I hadn't heard about that."

"I'm pretty sure she's all but forgotten about it. Honestly, if ever a gal could get over things and move on, it would be her."

"You do know them well, don't you?"

She smiled and laughed. "Yes. I'm also married to Macklin. So, as he is a member of Mason's team," she murmured, "that puts me in the inner circle for many things."

He smiled at that. "Nice to know you are part of Mason's extended family."

"Still enforcing the laws and keeping order in this city," she stated.

He chuckled. "I didn't need the reminder, but thank you."

Her grin flashed. "Just making sure."

"As you should," he said, with a nod. "In the meantime, what kind of reception can I expect from the family?"

"The worst. If you're planning on talking to them, expect to get kicked out. And, if they realize that you're on Mason's side, you might even be facing the barrel of a shotgun." He stared at her in surprise, and she nodded. "Trust me on this that no love is lost from that group now."

"Can you tell me anything about the family?"

"Self-made megamillionaires. Granddad set up some junkyards way back when, and he slowly built it up into a huge business, and now also owns grocery stores across the country."

"The dead kid's father is the only son to Granddad?"

"Son-in-law, one of two," she clarified. "And unfortunately the family pretty much babied the kid the entire time, so he had no challenges in life, which is why, as soon as Mason challenged him, the kid thought that would be one of his ultimate thrills. I think this was when he thought maybe he'd step it up to a killing, maybe with a rape of Tesla while he made Mason watch the rape." Guilliam let out a slow exhale at that. She nodded. "Just so you realize that the family doesn't believe the kid was guilty, and certainly didn't think anything of his crimes."

"We went through all of Mason's military cases, and, sure, there have been multiple killings, but again they were all classified as good kills."

"It doesn't matter how something is classified. When somebody thinks their loved one was treated unfairly, it's a done deal, and you'll never convince them otherwise."

"It's sad, isn't it?" he murmured. "A lot of people were hurt by his kid's actions."

"We had almost a dozen B&E cases that we feel were all his intrusions," she noted.

"So, how did Mason know it was him?"

"He got a bit of a description from his friend, and then he had an inkling over something the kid said during one of our interrogations." She stopped and then frowned. "I think the father or maybe the grandfather had a military connection, and that just set off the kid. Whatever he said got Mason's attention, something about somebody in the military would take care of things."

"So, he was counting on somebody else in the navy looking after him as well?"

"Seems like it, but I don't really know because that military connection never did get clarified. And I don't have anybody to clarify it now either."

"And who else is in this family tree?"

"I've lived here long enough to know something about that bunch. The grandfather is the oldest living patriarch. His wife died some years ago, and they have two daughters. He favored one over the other, as he loves to pit people against each other, even in his own bloodline. Both daughters married, and both had one child, each a son. The one Mason killed was the old man's favorite, of course."

"Is everybody left in the old man's family in good health?"

"No, the favored daughter is undergoing cancer treatment, so she's not in very good health. I understand her husband blames all this stress for creating her condition. So, what you're heading into, if you're planning on talking to them, is sure to be aggressive and all negative."

"Got it," he noted. "I may have to delay a face-to-face with them. Don't want to give them a heads-up that we're looking at them. Still, it would have been nice if the B&E kid would have thought about the repercussions of that before he headed down this pathway."

"Wouldn't it? But, with no challenges growing up, no guardrails, he didn't have to study, didn't have to work, didn't have to do anything. Trust-fund kid."

"And yet you would think they would be planning ahead, so he would have the skill set needed to take over the family business one day."

"Not sure Dad was prepared to make that happen, and the kid probably realized it wouldn't happen for a long time, so he figured he had time anyway. That's if he thought about it at all. It's not as if he's ever needed to do anything in his entire life."

"Crap." Guilliam got up. "Thanks for the heads-up."

She added, "You also need to be aware that, if anything happens, and I get called in to deal with you"—she eyed him pointedly—"there won't be any special treatment."

He gave her a bright toothy smile. "And that I appreciate."

She shook her head, a wry smile on her face. "You're all the same, aren't you?"

"Hey, Tesla's a very good friend of mine," he noted, "and I count Mason as one of my best friends in the world. So, if I can do anything to make this all stop, to resolve the continuing threat to Mason, and to stop the escalating body count, I'm all in."

She nodded. "I did hear from Jasper that the head count's gone up," she murmured. "If anybody crosses onto my side of that base, I'll be all over it."

"And that's possible," Guilliam replied. "No idea whether it will or won't, but I'll do my best to keep it on the base."

She laughed. "You're not doing me any favors if you do because Macklin's already involved in the background, as far as I can tell." She snorted. "I'm quite happy to help resolve all this properly, and once and for all."

"Sure, but you also know that, when things go to shit, nobody's worrying about location."

"I think the kid went to the base on purpose."

"Why is that?"

"He had the means to get in and out because of his grandfather's company. I think he used the company vehicle to access the base, and I think that, while he was there, he took a lot of ribbing because he was a spoiled little rich boy."

"Do you think he ever applied to the military?"

"If he did, it would have been squashed by Dad, I'm sure, but Dad will never admit to that."

"No, of course not," Guilliam stated. "Interesting, all this family history. I appreciate it."

"While the family history is interesting, it's not necessarily beneficial."

"It might explain why he went onto base to target Mason though."

She frowned and asked, "Why?"

"Because it would have been more of a challenge. Anything that happens on the base is a whole different story. The fact that you managed to close these home burglary cases because he was caught on base, and the case was closed at the time, obviously in conjunction with you, means there's got to be an awful lot of hate directed at you as well."

"There is an awful lot of hate directed at me regardless. Of course I'm an elected official, and that'll be coming home to roost before long," she stated, with a nod.

"Are you expecting to not get re-elected?"

"Not if that family has any say in the matter," she replied. "That's just a given."

"Got it, but I'm sure the rest of the town is happy that

the home invasions are over."

"Sure, but not everybody believes it was the kid. Quite a few don't have any problem seeing it that way though. Another thing that you may not be aware of is that this all happened quite a few years ago." When he frowned, she nodded. "Pretty sure it's been"—she looked down at the notes in her hand—"four years."

"Four years," he repeated. "Why would anybody wait four years?"

She sighed. "That's what I'm hoping you can tell me because, if it's dear old dad on a vendetta, he's waited a hell of a long time for his revenge. So, why now? And if not him, who else?"

Great questions, and ones he had no answers for.

CHAPTER 4

JANELLE MADE A quick trip home, had a shower, and changed. By the time she was back, her mother had been moved to the new room. She sat down beside her and whispered, "It's okay, Mom."

Her mother's eyes opened briefly, and she stared at her without recognition.

She smiled at her and whispered, "I'm here. I'm right here."

Her mother didn't even nod. She just seemed to drift in and right back out again.

With a sigh, Janelle settled in to watch over her mother.

The nurse walked in and asked, "How are you doing?"

"I'm okay. It just seems interminable."

"It is. Absolutely. You want it to go by faster, then you feel terribly guilty when you realize you're hoping for someone to hurry up and die."

"*Ugh.*" She looked over at her with a shrug. "And I don't want her to die at all, but this pain that she's going through is so hard to watch that I don't want it to continue for another minute."

The nurse smiled and nodded. "Don't let guilt get to you. Some things in life you can change, and others you cannot. So just adjust as much as you can and be there for her when she's awake. You should be good in here. We are still getting her into hospice though."

Janelle just nodded and didn't say anything because the thought of her mother being moved yet again didn't seem likely. It seemed more like she was now in a very tiny corner of the hospital, where people were prepared to wait her out. It sounded terrible, but Janelle was under the impression that hospitals always had a complete shortage of beds, so this waiting element didn't necessarily make sense to her from a for-profit hospital viewpoint.

And again nobody seemed to care. She had her ideas, and everybody else had theirs, as far as she could tell. But it also wasn't in her to judge. She was grateful they had taken a moment to move her mother as it was. And now that the move was completed and her mother was back to sleep again, Janelle could hopefully settle down and relax. She had brought a lot of work with her. Using a small lap table, she sat down, hoping to get some work done.

When Jasper popped by a little later, she looked up at him and smiled. "We got this much done. Mom is in a new room."

He nodded. "Any sign of your fake doctor person?"

She shook her head. "No, not at all."

"Good."

"Is it good though?" she asked in a wry tone.

"Yeah, because, if he finds you, it could be for all the wrong reasons, so chin up." He looked around and noted, "We tried to get you located away from the normal hospital rooms, but still where you could call out for help if you needed to."

"Oh my, I hadn't even considered that."

He laughed. "You can thank Guilliam for that."

She nodded, her smile falling away.

Jasper added, "It sounded like you were hoping to be friends again."

"Honestly, I would like to be a whole lot more than friends with him again," Janelle replied. "I made some tough decisions back then and chose to take care of my mother." She cast a glance back at the frail woman in the hospital bed. "How do you walk away from a woman who devoted her life to you? So, when she gets sick, you need to decide on what you will do. I decided to focus 100 percent of my attention on my mother. What I didn't think through at the time was that I didn't need to stop or abandon every other aspect of my life to do that. That was the mistake I made," she admitted. "And, yes, I do believe I'm paying for it."

He nodded but didn't say anything.

"It would be nice if he would forgive me."

"I'm not sure if forgiveness is the issue. I think it's probably trust. Realizing that, when push comes to shove, you're not number one is difficult because chances are, if something comes up again, you won't be number one again. So how can you ever be okay with *not* being number one, when you feel like you should be, even in a circumstance like this?" he shared, with a smile. "I do know that he was head over heels in love with you."

"Yeah. And that's what hurts."

He shrugged. "Everything takes a bit of time. He did arrange for you to be moved here, so he's certainly not indifferent."

"Maybe. And maybe he's just making sure that, if I have any other information, I'm ready and available to give it to you," she quipped.

He asked, "Do you?"

"I don't think so. I get that it's not something to joke about, yet it's hard to understand just what else I could offer," she said. "You know who the fake doctor is now. So I'm sure you're looking for him. He's got a record, or at least I presume he does, since he's known to you and in a mug-shot book already. He's bound to have an unsavory past of some kind."

Jasper nodded, then brought out a picture and asked, "Do you know this man?"

She looked at it and frowned. "No."

"If you see him, let us know immediately."

"Sure," she agreed, taking another look at the picture. "Any particular reason?"

"Just somebody of interest, but not necessarily in a nega-tive way. So, if you do see him, I don't want you approaching him."

She winced. "Right. That again."

"Yes, that again," he declared, his voice hardening. "We can't have that."

"Right. Fine, fine, fine," she muttered, with a wave of her hand. "I'm just staying out of everything at this point."

"Yeah, let me know how that works." He laughed.

"You don't think I can?"

"No, I'm not sure you can," he replied, "because I think your wanting to help wasn't so much about helping, as much as it was about finding a way to be useful to Guilliam, so that he would at least talk and pay attention to you."

She sucked in her breath and stared.

"I know that may feel like a low blow, and I don't mean it that way," he explained, "but it is something that you may want to consider." And, with that, he nodded and left.

As low blows went, it was definitely hard-hitting. Was he right? Maybe. She certainly hadn't thought of it that way, but she did want to be friends with Guilliam again, if that were possible. She truly wanted more than that. She wanted to go back to what they had—or rather build something to replace what they had. She just wasn't sure how to do that. Their breakup was all her fault for the decision she'd made, and she hadn't given him a chance to convince her otherwise.

She'd been so righteous in her need to help her mother that she had ignored the suggestion that what she was doing was wrong—even when it came from that very same mother Janelle was trying to help. Something about that need to pay back—or maybe it was a need to be needed. She didn't know. It just seemed as if everything had been so messed up for so long, and there wasn't much she could do about it. She returned her attention to her work, was on the phone several times, and when she looked up at one point, her mother was staring at her.

She hopped up, walked over, and asked, "Hey, how're you feeling?"

"Like I've got one foot on either side."

She sucked in her breath at that and sat down beside her mom. "I'm going to be fine when you go. You know that, right?"

Her mother patted her hand. "I know you will be, especially if Guilliam's back."

"He's back, but that doesn't mean he's back *with me*."

Her mother snapped, "Then you need to fix that."

"Not sure I can," she muttered. "I hurt him pretty badly."

Her mother just nodded and closed her eyes.

Janelle repeated, "Don't you worry about it, Mom. I'll deal with it."

Her mother's lips twitched. "Sure, but you have a tendency to deal with it through avoidance." And, with that, her mom drifted back to sleep again.

That was another one of those hard-to-handle truths. Two of them right after each other. Janelle sat there for a long time, and then, because she couldn't focus on work, she brought up her journal and wrote down everything that she needed to deal with in terms of Guilliam. Could she live with the fact that he may not be interested in getting back together with her? And what would that look like for her, outside of painful?

Somehow she'd always just assumed, in the back of her mind, that he would be there. That whenever she got her shit together, whenever this trial was over, she could call him up and would step right back into the relationship that they'd had before.

What she hadn't expected was for this process with her mother to take as long as it had because they had been looking at her getting over this, the cancer, not succumbing to it after a long and valiant struggle, which is where they were at now. And, therefore, the process had taken way longer than Janelle had expected. Despite the hope for the future, she had been tucked away. No way she could have asked him to wait for her all this time. For all she knew, he'd already had half a dozen other relationships. That thought would crush her if she let it, yet she had no right to expect he had not.

She was the one who'd hurt him. She was the one who had chosen to walk away from him. And that sucked. When she was finally done pouring out all her emotions onto the page, she realized her throat was parched from crying in soft, quiet sobs that she hoped nobody had heard. Not that anybody would care because so many people here were dealing with their own pain and struggles. So a woman crying at the bedside of her mother shouldn't have caused shock or surprise for anybody else. Not that she wanted anybody to witness her anguish.

She quickly dried her tears and walked over and gave her mom a kiss. "I will go get a cup of tea."

And, with that, she put her laptop and her journal into her bag, tucked it on the far side of the bed, a habit she'd gotten into because leaving something out didn't seem like the smartest idea, and then she headed down to the cafeteria. She stopped in at the ladies' room first and gave her face a good wash, spruced up her hair, and even went so far as to smack her cheeks to put some color back into them. Nothing quite like looking after a dying person to make everything else fall apart. Then she headed to the cafeteria, where she managed to smile, as she moved her way through to get her tea.

When she had finally paid for it and was heading back up to the room, one of the nurses stopped her and whispered, "Your mother had another episode."

She froze in fear.

The nurse added, "She's okay at the moment but ..."

"Right." Janelle turned and raced to her mom's room. As she walked in, a doctor stood there, studying her chart. "I just went to get a cup of tea."

He gave her half a smile. "All it takes is just a few minutes away. Sometimes they don't want to pass away while you're here."

"She's alive then. She's okay?"

He hesitated, then spoke. "Yes, but I don't think hospice will be an option anymore. This move, if anything, has highlighted that she's, … she's almost gone."

"And I don't suppose you wanna hazard a guess as to how long she has."

He shook his head. "If I give you my best guess, chances are, I'll be wrong, but I will hazard a guess anyway and hope that you have at least that much time. I suspect she will go in the next twenty-four to forty-eight hours." And, with that, he gave a small nod and walked out.

She stepped out in the hallway and watched him leave, the tears already streaming from her eyes. With death that close, the time to be with her mother was truly fleeting. She needed to be with her as much as she could, as much as anybody could, and yet knew that it won't be nearly enough time. Somehow they'd hit the end of the road, … and now Janelle knew it. She'd known it was coming. There's no way she hadn't, but supposedly knowing it was a whole different story than living it and having it pointed out in terms as specific as a number of hours.

As she walked back inside, she stopped, and feeling an odd sense, she turned to see a man walking quickly down the hallway in a white coat. She froze as she recognized the tilt of the head and pulled out her phone and contacted Guilliam.

"He was just here," she said softly. "As in, I think he just saw me."

"I'M ON MY way. I was heading to the hospital already, so I'll be there in a few minutes. Just go in and stay with your mother and remember that you're not alone." And, with that, Guilliam hung up.

As far as getting to the bottom of this Mason sniper shooting, Guilliam hadn't had a chance to do anything so far but drive past the dead intruder's family home, realizing it was a very large estate with big locked gates outside. Guilliam wasn't sure who even lived in the home. He understood that the owner's wife was in cancer treatment, but he didn't know at what stage her cancer might be in.

As he headed to the hospital entrance, it occurred to him that it was possible this vengeful rich guy might have a legitimate reason for being at the hospital. Not for impersonating a doctor, if that's what he was doing. It wasn't that Guilliam doubted Janelle, but he did recognize that she was not in the best mental state, considering what was going on in her world.

As he stepped into her new hospital room, he saw Miriam open her eyes and stare in his direction. He stepped closer and picked up her hand. He carried it to his lips and kissed it.

She gave him a ghost of a smile. "You did come."

"I came."

"Just in time," she murmured.

He shrugged. "I don't know about that, but I'm here, and it seems like maybe it's time for you to relax and to let go."

Her eyes widened, and she nodded. "And maybe I can, now that I know you're here."

"But you knew I was here before," he said.

"Yes, but I just didn't *know*-know."

He looked over to see Janelle in the doorway, staring from the hallway. Whether she heard them or not, he didn't know, but it was obvious that her mother had something that she needed to say.

"I'm so grateful that you're here for her now."

He didn't want to correct her, so he didn't say anything.

Miriam nodded. "I saw the way you looked at her."

He leaned over and whispered, "I know, but it's not that easy."

Her lips twitched, and, with great effort, she whispered right back, "It's not that hard either." Then she closed her eyes and fell back asleep again.

Guilliam waited a moment to confirm that her chest was still rising, realizing what Janelle had been through, going through this ordeal on a daily basis, for all this time. When he straightened up and walked toward Janelle, he saw the tears in her eyes.

She whispered, "The doctor said it would be twenty-four to forty-eight hours."

He wasn't sure it would even be that long and thought it was almost like Miriam was letting go, now that she had seen him. He nodded and whispered, "And maybe that's for the best."

"It is for the best," she conceded, as she turned to look back at her mother, "but that doesn't make it easy."

"No, of course not," he whispered. "How are you holding up?"

She shrugged. "Terribly. I'm a wreck, but I guess this isn't something I'm supposed to excel at."

His lips twitched at her caustic tone, and he nodded. "You could be right."

She groaned. "I'm sorry. I'm not trying to be difficult."

"Listen. You're entitled to be snappish and off guard and fed up and upset. You're in the process of saying goodbye to somebody who really matters to you."

At his wording, Janelle's tears started to flow again. She sobbed. "I'm sorry. I'm so sorry. I keep telling myself I'm not doing this."

With that, he just pulled her into his arms and held her. As she sagged against him and bawled, he understood the devastation that was going on in her life. She'd made a lot of decisions regarding care for her mother, and, as much as he understood why she had left him behind, it had still hurt terribly at the time. He just held her close, gently rubbing her back.

When she finally ran out of tears, she mumbled, "I'm sorry. I keep thinking I won't cry anymore. I keep thinking I'm done with the tears, and then something happens, and I just can't hold it together."

"You don't have to hold it together all the time, you know," he muttered. "Don't expect too much of yourself right now."

She looked over at him. "And yet that seems wrong too."

"And why is that? Remember that your mother has been there through all of it, and, while her body may be worn out, her constitution is strong. She's caring, she's capable, and … she's ready to go."

"I know, but that doesn't make the process any easier."

He nodded. "I'm not trying to make it sound like it's less than it is," he murmured. "Obviously going through what you're experiencing is probably the hardest thing anybody has to go through. I just want you to look after yourself in the process."

"I'll look after myself … *after* I've finished looking after my mother."

CHAPTER 5

JANELLE DIDN'T WANT to belabor the point, but it was hard for her to get anybody else to understand, and that bothered her too. Still, she'd made her decision a long time ago, and she would finish her job as her mother's caretaker. As she sat at her mother's side, she knew that Guilliam had gone to check something with hospital security. Probably the cameras to see where that fake doctor guy was. She couldn't be as sure this time, having not seen him as clearly as she had before. Yet was he hiding away in this section of the hospital or at least staying away from her. So why was he taking so many chances?

Surely if he was going after Mason, it would be a quick in-and-out thing. The fact that he may be waiting for an opening was also concerning. The last thing she wanted was for Mason to get hit again. Tesla didn't deserve that, and neither did Mason. He was a good guy. And to think that these assholes were ruining everybody's lives just pissed her off again. As she sat here and waited, her mother murmured something.

She got up and walked over to her bed. "I didn't hear you, Mom. Did you need something?"

Her mother's eyes opened wide, and Janelle stared for a

moment, then saw a familiar beaming smile. It had been such a long time since she had seen one. She looked down at her mother, both awestruck and emotional at the serene beauty in her mother's face.

"He came back for you," Mom whispered. "I can leave in peace now."

"Whoa, whoa, whoa, what are you talking about?"

Janelle felt a squeeze of her fingers, as she watched in shock, while her mother's eyes closed, and she stopped breathing. She stared down at her mother, stunned, waiting for that gasping breath that would say her mother was still here, that she had lived through whatever this nightmare was. It didn't come, and it didn't come, and it didn't come. When it finally hit her that it wouldn't ever come again, she burst into tears and bent down to hug her mother's frail body, knowing that she was gone, yet unable to let go. When she felt strong warm arms pick her up, she knew Guilliam was back again. He sat her down in his lap off to the side, while she cried.

She lifted her head and stared up at him, and he whispered, "It's okay. Let it go. Let it out. You're fine. You need to do this."

And, without warning, she once again burst into tears and bawled, thankful for the security of his embrace. When she finally lay quiet against his chest, her body still trembling, he just held her. She could see her mother lying there, her face peaceful in death.

Janelle shook her head. "She smiled up at me and said something very odd."

He looked down at her, his gaze warm and caring.

"She said, *He came back for you. Now I can go in peace.*" He stiffened for a moment and then relaxed. She looked up at him. "She didn't contact you, did she?"

He lowered his gaze, then nodded. "She told me that her time was coming," he murmured.

She pushed back off his lap somewhat, but he held her firm. "And you came?" she asked in astonishment.

He shrugged. "I was asked to come for another reason as well."

"Mason?"

He nodded.

"So, it was a timing thing, more than anything. Or are you telling me that you wouldn't have come if Mom hadn't called?"

His lips twitched. "I don't know how to answer that because I didn't have the opportunity to experience that," he admitted. "I came. That's what's important."

She nodded, and, unable to do anything else, she sagged against him. "You don't have to feel obligated."

He squeezed her and replied, "That's not my style."

"No, but, in a case like this, I can see you feeling that way."

He didn't say anything, just continued to rub her back.

She leaned into his familiar touch. "How long has it been?" she murmured.

"Three years," he replied. "Three years, three months, and twelve days."

She stiffened, then pulled back and stared at him.

He nodded. "I knew that I had to step back to let you do what you needed to do," he explained, "but that didn't make it easy on me."

"And you kept track?" she asked in a daze.

He nodded. "I kept track because I knew, at one point in time, you would need me, or you would at least be open to seeing me again."

"I never stopped wanting to see you. I never stopped wanting to have you in my life, but I just needed to focus on Mom."

"And I understand that," he said.

"Good, because now obviously isn't the time to even talk about it, but—"

The nurse walked in, interrupting them. She sighed, walked over to her mom, and stated, "She looks so peaceful."

And for that Janelle was grateful.

The nurse turned to look at the pair of them and asked, "You want a few minutes with her?"

Immediately Janelle nodded. "If you wouldn't mind."

The nurse smiled. "That's fine. We can give you a little bit of time. There's also a chapel down the hallway, if you want to go spend some time there."

Janelle, almost numb, nodded. As soon as the nurse was gone, she looked up at Guilliam. "I would like to stay with her for a bit to say goodbye somehow."

He nodded. "I will give you some privacy. I'll be back in half an hour."

She nodded, already moving toward the hospital bed. Looking up at him, she whispered, "Thank you."

He nodded. "You don't need to thank me. Thank your mom." And, with that, he was gone.

GUILLIAM HEADED STRAIGHT to the security office. As soon as he knocked, the door opened, and he was let in. Obviously phone calls had been made back and forth to give him access now.

As he walked in, one of the men pointed to a work-station set up on the side. "We've loaded the cameras for you."

He sat down and quickly sorted through the ones he wanted, and it didn't take long to pick out the man Janelle had mentioned. Guilliam studied it for a moment, then nodded. "That's him again."

"The same man you saw earlier?"

"Yes. This time he's not wearing a doctor's white lab coat but a janitor's outfit."

The security men looked at it and nodded. One guy said, "I'll send out an alert, but he's probably long gone."

Guilliam frowned. "Maybe not. You do what you need to do. I'm heading up to the room that we have guarded."

"You've got Mason in there, don't you?"

He looked over at him and nodded. "Do you know him?"

"Sure do. I've been volunteering to be security as well."

"We'll figure out who's behind it, hopefully soon. Apparently several years back Mason's home was the scene of a home invasion, and Mason ended up shooting the guy."

The security guard nodded. "I remember that. It was that punk-ass kid and good riddance. Besides, it was a clean kill."

"Absolutely clean," Guilliam confirmed, "but we're wondering if somebody in that family is holding a grudge."

"I wouldn't be at all surprised," the guard noted, staring off in the distance. "That family is very patriarchal. Just so you know, I wouldn't even put it past the grandfather."

"Is the grandfather still living?" Guilliam asked.

"He is, but he's in an old folks home. The man is still a power unto himself though. The shit these people get away with because they've got money just drives me nuts."

"Enough to do something like hiring a sniper to kill Mason and then a follow-up killer to finish him off in a hospital?"

The guard raised his eyebrow. He looked back at the cameras and muttered, "I wouldn't be at all surprised. They don't think the rules apply to them. That's why Gabe was never caught. I sincerely believe that he just bullied people into keeping quiet and giving terrible descriptions of who he was and what he was doing. This may be Greg, the other grandson, but I haven't seen him in a long time. Maybe he's now the bully, the muscle, behind the old coot."

"That would imply he had some form of leverage, if he could apply that pressure."

"His family is one of the biggest employers in town, and the grandfather was the guy who initially would threaten them with layoffs, threaten them with broken legs and all kinds of shit. Then as he got older, I guess Gabe took over as head bully. I don't even know what got him started with the B&Es, but I wouldn't be surprised if it was a dare for him."

"Somebody mentioned a lack of challenges in Gabe's life."

"Yeah, you're not kidding. He got everything handed to him, talk about advertising for better parenting," he muttered. "I've got kids, and no way in hell I would ever let my kids get away with crap like that."

"Too often it seems to be the parents' fault, but sometimes it can be other influences too."

"That's what I meant about patriarchal. The mother didn't have a whole lot of say in anything going on. She was one of those very pretty arm-candy types. Nice-enough lady, always involved in the schools, charity work, and things like that, but you didn't get any idea of who she was because she wasn't around much. The men were the main presence in the family. Strong-arm all-male types who had power and weren't above using it."

"Right. Now I need to figure out where the family is these days."

"I thought Greg and his mom moved out of state. I'm not sure where. Although that sure looks like him in that janitor's uniform. They were the black sheep of the family. The family in general didn't believe the killing of Gabe was justified and held Mason to blame for it. But, as you mentioned, that was a lot of years ago to hold a grudge before acting on it."

"So, the question is, what would stir that all up again?"

"I don't know if anything would, unless they were just waiting for everybody to let down their guard, thinking it was long over and done, then seizing their chance to drop Mason where he stood."

At the phrase, Guilliam turned to face the guard. "Interesting phrase."

"Gabe and the granddad are those kind of guys. They were that kind of family. The kind to fire people publicly and to humiliate them at the same time. There's no love lost for that family in this town, yet Greg or his granddad could still coerce some needy local to finish off Mason. The problem is, they need somebody with skills and somebody who can navigate around all the security we've got on Mason. Regardless, the grandfather would have had a scapegoat to make sure they wouldn't get blamed—or at least the old coot wouldn't get blamed."

"An awful lot of people are involved in this deal, mostly dead now, and it seems the mastermind behind it all had some blackmail material to get people motivated to do whatever he wanted."

"My guess would be the grandfather. He's a mafia wannabe, using threats to keep his employees in line. He's the kind of guy who would put cameras everywhere to collect information, pay kids to sit in the pool halls to get the dirt on people. I can also tell you that they've also had long arms into the military."

Guilliam stiffened. Just another reminder of the secret investigation taking place into the high-level brass within the navy, who already seem to be bought and paid for. Guilliam sighed loudly.

The guard asked Guilliam, "You do know all the shit that goes on there, right? Please tell me that you're not thinking it's all innocent."

"No, I'm not. I'm perfectly aware that shit goes on at the base that shouldn't."

"The kid was always blabbing about how he had lots of contacts and that he could make things happen."

"Of course." Guilliam swore. "And people would believe the spoiled rich kid."

"They didn't have a whole lot of choice because, well, he's just a power-mad bully, and his grandfather hired a lot of townspeople in his business."

"Nice."

"No, definitely not," the guard said, with a laugh. "But things calmed down after Gabe died. The grandfather was angry, very angry, for a long time. He fired a lot of people, seemingly for no reason. That was the thing that got to people because it was just like he was pissed off and wanted to make everyone else pay. He hated the world."

"*Nice,*" Guilliam muttered, realizing just what a shit this guy was.

"And the thing is, everybody did pay. They paid in a big way."

"What about Gabe's father?"

The guard frowned. "He's not like his father-in-law or Gabe, not even before Gabe died. He was the professional face of the company, in suits, taking meetings. However, once Gabe died, I think his father died inside too. Plus, then suddenly Gabe's mother was in cancer treatment. She travels into the city all the time to see her oncologist but then comes back home to recuperate. Everybody treats her gently, and I don't believe there's any hostility toward her. Again she's not been near the problem that her father and then her son were."

"Of course, though that doesn't mean that she couldn't be dangerous in her own way."

"Agreed, but I just don't think that's near the top of her list of things to be worried about right now."

"Is she likely to make it?"

"I don't know. I haven't heard the latest. In fact I can't say I've heard very much in the way of gossip about her lately."

"*Huh*. That makes sense. Whatever's going on in her world, I'm sure it's completely dominated by her cancer treatments."

"You would think so," the guard replied. "I can't imagine what she's going through, honestly. I've been blessed with good health and so has the bulk of my family. But, if you were employed at the family's grocery stores, and you needed a few days off so you could get a family member some care that they needed or something else, the grandfather was that asshole who would charge you for your time off, make you acutely aware that he was doing it as a gift, and in some cases make you work double just to get your job back."

Shaking his head, Guilliam snorted. "The fact that nobody has killed him is what's surprising to me," Guilliam noted. "An asshole like that, you would think somebody would have taken him out long ago."

"I think, if people weren't so terrified, they would have. The apple doesn't fall far from the tree. And while the old man is in a home, I highly doubt he's any less dangerous at this stage of his life than he was before." The guard gave a headshake. "He just orders it done from the old folks' home. The whole family is vengeful like that."

"Good to know. I think I'll go pay him a visit."

"You do that, because the more I look at this image, I'm more convinced that this is Greg, the other grandson."

"He appears to be, yes."

The guard nodded. "Yeah, it could be a cousin maybe, or who knows? Maybe there are more grandkids that I don't know about. This is probably your closest connection to that family," he murmured. "In which case I sure as hell hope you get the whole lot of them."

"Do you really think they would be behind something like this?"

"Oh, absolutely. They would definitely do something like this," he declared, with a hard nod. "And they would make sure whoever carried out the deed knew what they were doing and why, and they would make sure they knew they had absolutely no choice."

"We have an awful lot of people who pissed him off," Guilliam noted. "So, it's a matter of whether all these pathways lead to this one guy and his family, or somewhere else."

"My vote is this family," the guard declared. "Until you've seen all the shit they do, you just don't understand how evil these assholes are."

"If the grandfather is old, maybe dying, could that be a push to exact revenge on Mason for Gabe's death? After all, it's been like four years since the kid died."

"Oh, yeah. The grandfather would want to see with his own eyes that it was done." And, with that, a buzzer went off. The security guard sighed. "Looks like I need to get back to work." And, with that, he quickly got up and left.

Guilliam took copies of the images and several photographs of the guy in action, and, with his notes, he headed back to the hospital room where Janelle was. As he got closer, he phoned Jasper and brought him up to date.

"That's exactly where my thoughts are too," Jasper stated. "I talked to our chatty prisoner again and brought up the name. He just nodded and didn't say a whole lot, but he reacted with almost a sense of relief."

"Your prisoner's probably being blackmailed. I don't think this is about money because these minions aren't getting paid. This rich guy seems to have something on just about every single person involved in Mason's case. Apparently he's the kind of guy who liked to keep track of everybody and every problem or indiscretion, so, if he ever needed to, he could apply a little pressure and make them do things."

"Nice guy. You would think somebody would have popped him by now."

At that, Gilliam laughed. "I just told the security guard the same damn thing. At least we have an angle to work. I want to get an address for the old folks' home for the grandfather, so I can see if the old man is prepared to talk. I'm hoping that, since he's closer to meeting his maker, maybe he'll be a little more willing to have a discussion."

"Chances are, he won't be. My money is on his being 100 percent family all the way."

"I wouldn't be at all surprised. That doesn't mean that he's not got some sense of decency in him though. And, if that fails, there's the sickly daughter."

"I hear she's recovering from or dealing with cancer treatments, so any visitation to her is likely to chew people up."

"If I need to speak to her, I'm not too bothered about that either," Guilliam stated, his voice firm. "We've got to get some answers, and we need them fast. If this cousin or whoever this relative is who's walking the hospital hallways is looking for a way to get through to Mason, you can bet that the family won't let this guy off the hook anytime soon."

"Maybe not," Jasper conceded, "but no way in hell we're letting that asshole get close enough for another attempt."

"You can say that, but we also know that these guys are slippery."

"I don't know if this hospital guy's got any training, but, if he thinks that he's got any way to make this happen, he will try it at some point."

"That's why we've got triple guards on Mason right now."

"I hear you, and that may be enough, but I won't believe it until we get that far."

"I'm not taking any chances either," Guilliam murmured. "But I do hear you, and I understand what we're up against. I'm more concerned that they have more threads to pull and more blackmail for somebody else in the military who's got the skills they need. I think this guy loitering in the hospital is into collecting blackmail info, just figuring out how they can make it happen, and then they'll decide who to call on to do the job."

"That would suck," Jasper replied, "because these guys feel as if they have absolutely no other choice, and you know how dangerous criminals can be when desperate."

"So, what are you thinking?"

"I think that Drew deliberately missed the shot and was probably hoping the bad guys who hired him would think it was an accident or that he couldn't get off a good-enough shot. He was planning to run anyway."

"And yet there was supposed to be money."

"But was there, or did he just tell his partner that, hoping he could get away with that too? We found one major deposit in one of Drew's accounts, if memory serves. But who's to say that the right guy didn't blackmail a hacker to doctor up Drew's account? Plus, we never found any money with Suzan. So that all lends credence to your *no*-money theory. It was all about blackmail instead. And maybe both Drew and Suzan were in on it," Jasper suggested.

Guilliam muttered, "You would like to think some decent people are out there somewhere, especially on a goddamn military base. To even have gone as far as shooting Mason says a lot," he murmured. "And none of it good. Drew obviously felt that he had zero choice in the matter and that this was the best option."

"If that's the case, I sure as hell am sorry that Drew is dead because I would have liked to have talked to him."

"Yeah, you and me both," Guilliam agreed. "I'm at Janelle's room now. Her mom passed away about thirty minutes ago. I left her to say her last goodbyes, while I went to the security room. I'm just about there now and will take her home after this. She's got a bunch of stuff to deal with and to arrange for her mom, but I'm hoping that, at some point in time, she will be ready to move on."

"Give her enough time to work through it though," he warned.

"Oh, I plan on it, don't worry. It's never been about pushing her. It was always about waiting for her," he admitted. "I'm just kind of glad that the wait's over. It was getting hard to wait."

"You really did come back for her, didn't you?"

"I came back for Mason, but it turned out to be perfect timing for both. I'm glad I didn't have to make that decision and choose between Mason and her."

"Nobody should ever have to make a decision between one or the other," he pointed out. "Life's hard enough without that."

"I agree," he murmured, "which is why I backed off and left her to look after her mother. It was something she clearly felt incredibly strongly about, so I wouldn't fight her on it."

"At the same time, I'm sure she felt that you deserted her."

"It was the other way around. She pushed me away in no uncertain terms," he shared, with a heavy sigh. "Anyway, her mom did call me a while back, and it wasn't all that long ago. I'm not sure whose phone she used, but she was certainly lucid enough on the phone at that time. I didn't realize that she was as close to the end as she was, but I did realize that she didn't have too much time or she wouldn't have called me."

"Sounds like she was very stubborn."

"Yeah, both of them are," he stated, with a laugh. Up

ahead, he saw the door to the room where Janelle was waiting. "Anyway, I'm here now. I'll give you a shout as soon as I've got her home. And I sent you the camera stills of the guy, and I need to—Can you find me the old folks' home where the grandfather stays and also wherever the daughter with cancer is? I'll go make those visits too."

"Good enough," Jasper said and ended the call.

Guilliam walked into her room and stopped. No sign of her. He looked around. Her bag was there but no sign of her. Frowning, he walked down to the nurses' station and asked if they had seen her. The nurse looked up and shook her head.

"I was giving her a few minutes before we came and removed her mother's body," she replied.

"And I gave her a few minutes, told her that I would be back in thirty." He checked his watch. "And I'm right on time."

"She may have gone to the washroom. She was pretty upset."

"That's a good point." He turned and headed to the washroom and then back to the hospital room again but still found no sign of her. He pulled out his phone and called her, and when it started to ring from the floor, where they'd been sitting, his heart sank. He walked around, picked up the phone, and realized absolutely no way she would have just left it behind willingly. And now he knew they had a kidnapping on their hands as well.

CHAPTER 6

J ANELLE GROANED AND reached up to hold her head, willing the pain of a booming headache to stop.

"Shut up," a man snapped at her. "If you bring any attention to us, I'll be pissed."

She slowly opened her eyes, not sure who was talking, but knowing it wasn't Guilliam. She stared at the face in front of her. "*Ugh*, … you."

"Yes, me," he declared, giving her a hard grin. "When I looked at things from a business perspective and realized that you would probably be the best ticket in this case, I couldn't believe my luck. You weren't on my list, until I realized you would be the ultimate leverage to get somebody to do something I needed him to do."

She swore at that. "I don't know what you think you're going to do, but now that my mother's gone, nobody out there will give a shit about me one way or another," she snapped.

"Oh, I think you're wrong there." He chuckled. "Maybe you don't quite believe it yet, but he cares. Oh, he cares a lot, and he'll pay dearly," he declared. "We need this to go away, and we needed something completed."

"What's the matter?" she asked, staring at him. "You run

out of lackeys?"

"Yeah, I did," he admitted. "And not just me, the whole family's got a problem with that right now. But apparently your boy Guilliam's a part of this bloody mess, and we were looking for a weakness to exploit, So guess what? You're it."

She shook her head. "Then you don't understand."

"Oh, I understand just fine," he stated. "You can say all you want, but it won't make a difference. It will be your life or Mason's."

She frowned at him, knowing that choice would kill Guilliam. "Then it will be my life," she decided. "You already know that."

"I hope you're wrong," he muttered, giving her a nasty look. "If it was me, it would be an easy choice. I would pop you in seconds." He glared at her. "But we need somebody to take care of business, and it looks to be you."

"And if I'm not?"

"Then you're in trouble because, if you're not it, I have to get rid of you anyway," he explained. "I can't let you live. So, don't even start with promises that you won't tell anybody, especially since you've already blabbed several times."

She winced and sighed at that because she had. She'd even accosted him in the hallway. "You were obviously not a doctor, and you were walking around this place, looking lost, like an idiot. It was clear you were up to something."

He glared at her. "Keep talking. Chances are good I'll have to pop you, and you're just making it all the more appealing."

"What do you mean, chances are good?" she asked. "It's more than chances. You've already told me how you can't let me live. So, no matter what I say, no matter what Guilliam does, you will kill me. Do you think he won't know that? No way will he play your stupid little game."

"He better," the fake doctor growled, "because, if you think you're the only one I can use for leverage, you're wrong. You'll just be the place I start. We'll see how quickly he falls into line, and, if not quickly enough, believe me that I'll just up the ante."

She stared at him, her stomach sinking as she realized he was prepared to kill her to ensure Mason died. "So, it doesn't matter to you about Mason, as long as he's dead, is that it?"

"Personally I would even be happy with him permanently being a vegetable," he shared, with a laugh. "I don't have a whole lot in this fight, but it matters to the family. Mason killed my cousin, so he's got to pay."

"And what about the fact that your cousin was trying to kill Mason's wife?"

"He didn't plan to kill her. He planned to rape her."

She stared at him in shock. "And that's okay with you?"

"No, but, when it comes to shit like that, and it's family, it is what it is," he told her. "And since the old man's due to die sometime soon, if I want to be in his will—and billions are in that estate—I have to do my part."

"And if you don't do your part?"

He shrugged. "Presumably I get cut out. At least that's been the threat since forever."

"Aren't you tired of getting your chain yanked?"

"Sure." He sent her a glare. "And that's another reason I'm not letting you mess up anything. He's almost dead."

She asked, "Your grandfather?"

He nodded. "See? That's why you'll get popped anyway. You know too much."

"You guys don't make it hard to figure out," she replied,

with a sneer.

He turned to face her. "Keep it up. Just keep it up. I may have to make you suffer before I kill you."

"See what it gets you," she taunted. Janelle wanted to shut up, she really did, but this part of her couldn't let anybody else yank her chain. She'd spent a lot of years doing what she thought was right, and it was right, and she wouldn't listen to anybody else telling her that it wasn't. She wasn't even that person anymore. She was free. She had done what she thought she needed to do, and she would never resent the time she spent helping her mother, but she would be damned if she'd let this guy ruin it for her now. "You do realize I spent the last three years nursing my mother, and now she's gone, as of about an hour ago. Now you're here, trying to take a new life away from me."

He barked out a laugh. "Yeah, that's pretty funny. You finally get a chance to live without the old broad, and here you are, about to get killed for something you didn't even do."

"I can see how that really bothers you too," she quipped.

He laughed and laughed. "Yeah, it does." Then his laughter cut off midstream, as he glared at her again. "All I give a shit about is making sure I get my share of that estate. The rest I don't give a crap about."

"Maybe you should go pop the old man instead."

"Oh, I've thought about it, don't you worry. And, if he keeps living much longer, I probably will." When she winced at that, he laughed. "You don't even like it when I tell you the truth."

"Wow. You are not a nice guy. Yet it's you, and you are whatever you are. I can't see that you're likely to give a crap about anyone else anytime soon, even your own violent family."

"No, I won't," he confirmed. "So, don't worry about it. And you sure as hell can't redeem me, so get that idea out of your head. I've been doing their bidding for a very long time, and for an even longer time they've been promising me all kinds of shit," he explained. "It's payday time, as soon as we've done this job. I've put an awful lot on the line for it, and I'm not missing out now."

"But that implies that you think you'll have a chance to spend that money," she noted, looking at him. "No way that's happening, especially not now."

"Sure, I will. What with Mason dead, and Guilliam doomed to die, those two are out of the way. … I expect you to burst into tears anytime now." He gave her an exaggerated eye roll. "What, no tears?"

He wore such a mocking expression that she just glared at him, hating the power in his tone, based on his belief that he held all the aces in his hand. "You have these grandiose ideas, yet you've been wandering this hospital for at least the two days that I first noticed you. If you have things all wrapped up, why the hell didn't you pop Mason two days ago? Why the hell didn't you shoot Guilliam two days ago? Why the hell didn't you kidnap me two days ago? Are you waiting for the real killer in your family to show up? Yet your cousin is dead, and your granddad is too old and infirm. So are you waiting for *Daddy* to come pull the trigger? You talk like you know it all. You don't know anything." She stared at him in fury.

"It's called *surveillance.*" He slapped her hard, rattling her teeth, and her headache bloomed again. "Shut your trap. In case you haven't noticed, you're sitting in a laundry hamper, and I will soon take you out of this hospital and move you someplace where nobody will find you."

She swallowed at hearing that, rubbing her jaw, hoping none of her teeth had been knocked loose with his slap.

He nodded. "Believe me when I say that nobody will hear you, that nobody will give a shit about you, once you're out of here. You've probably been a pain in the ass to the nurses since the day your mother arrived, and then you just moved in too. God, how disgusting to stay at the hospital while she was dying," he said. "That's just gross."

Shocked at his attitude, she asked, "What I did was gross, but killing people for money isn't?"

"No, that's just business."

"*Right.* My vote is you get your ass kicked before you end up with your cousin."

He glared at her. "That's not happening."

"You don't think the rest of your screwed-up family will throw you to the wolves? Of course they will. That's the kind of family you belong to, right? Nobody gives a shit about you. They just want to make sure that whatever they're doing happens, and then you'll be blamed," she pointed out, with a broad smile. "I wouldn't get too happy as you dream about that inheritance money because I don't see any of it coming your way, or, if it does, it will be temporary, and you'll be dead before you get a chance to spend it."

The hand that smacked her across the face again had dealt a blow before, but even now she smiled as she looked at him, knowing she'd gotten his goat. She knew what made him tick. Clearly the thought that he wouldn't get his payday and that the family might somehow turn the tables on him was enough to make him choke. She continued to smile at him. "Nice to know you can lose control too."

"Yeah, I hope so because the next time I lose control, it

might just be with a bullet. Now shut up."

"And if I don't?"

He sighed. "You know what? This will be easier." And, with that, he pushed the laundry cart into the wall, slamming her head hard against the concrete, and she blacked out.

GUILLIAM YELLED INTO the phone, "She's gone. Her phone's here and all the rest of her stuff, but she's gone."

Jasper replied, calm and stable, "That doesn't mean she's not in the bathroom."

"I checked," he snapped. "I'm heading back to security right now."

"Good idea."

"We'll send out an alert within the hospital and make sure she's not still on the premises somewhere," he said.

"See what you can find from security. I'm on my way." And then Jasper ended the call.

Guilliam turned the last corner, approaching the security unit, when his phone rang. Hearing the man on the other end, he slowed his steps. "Who is this?"

"Somebody who has a package that you care about," said the guy in a mocking tone.

He stopped. "If you touch her, I'll kill you, you little bastard."

"Ooh, look at that, feisty words. You must be missing somebody. Not very good at your job, since you allowed her to get plucked away from you."

He glared into his phone. "What do you want?"

"I want a lot of things in life, but the big question is,

what do I need? And what I need is for you to finish the job on Mason."

He froze. "That won't happen."

"If it doesn't," he replied in a mocking tone. "you'll never see her alive again." And, with that, the call was terminated.

Guilliam stared down at his cell, his breathing raspy and horrified. He phoned Jasper. "The kidnapper just contacted me," he began, his voice harsh. "They want me to finish the job on Mason."

"What?"

"Yeah."

"Holy shit. What the hell is going on here?" Jasper asked.

"This is an all-out deal against Mason, I gather," Guilliam replied.

"I'm on the way. I'll grab Masters and Gideon and get the whole team there."

"I don't even know if she's still here in the hospital," Guilliam noted. "I have no idea where she is. I don't know how long she's been missing. I'm at the security door right now."

"Follow up, get that going. I'll get everybody there. We've got police out looking for the fake doctor as well."

"Yeah, you might have the police out, but he's got her," he declared, his throat constricting. "God, what have I done?"

"You've done nothing, man," Jasper stated. "You remember that. This asshole has done this. Not you."

"You say that, but—"

"I mean it," he snapped. "You and I both know these guys are just looking for opportunities to prey on somebody like her."

"Exactly," Guilliam grumbled, "and, if I hadn't shown her that I was here, if I hadn't looked after her—"

Jasper interrupted, "Then somebody else would be their kidnap victim. You and I both know that it's much better that this involves you, that this involves us. We can deal with this," he stated. "Hang on, and get the damn hospital security team on it."

"I'm here. I'll call you back." He quickly disconnected and raced inside, barking off orders. When the security guards realized what had gone on, everybody began searching through the various cameras to see what happened.

"He's right there," one of the guards yelled, pointing at one of the cameras in the hallway. "He's pushing a laundry cart."

"Where's the laundry room?" Guilliam snapped.

"Down in the second basement," he replied.

"Okay, I'm heading down there. Keep tracking him, see where he and that cart goes, and somebody call me as soon as you find anything," he cried out, as he raced from the room.

The security guard he'd spoken to earlier joined him. "Come on. I know where we're going, so I can get you there faster. This way." He quickly ran down to a double set of elevators. "We need to go on the industrial one."

And, with him at Guilliam's side, they ran until they were at the laundry room. Guilliam stopped and looked around, while the security guard talked to the rest of his team on his phone, with the Speaker on. "A couple carts are here," the guard shared, "but no sign of anybody in them."

"Where did he go?" Guilliam roared. "You should be on those cameras right now. Where did he go?"

"We're checking. We're checking," the other guard replied from the phone. "We're not seeing anything."

"He didn't just pick her up and carry her over his shoulder out of here," Guilliam snapped. At least he didn't think the kidnapper would. "Would you have noticed? Do you ever get anybody carrying something suspicious like that?"

"Not like that," the guard beside Guilliam noted. "But if some guy was carrying a suitcase or a duffel bag, obviously that would be something suspicious. What do you guys see?" he asked the guards in the security room.

The guard on the phone replied, "We're looking, but we're not seeing anything yet."

"Keep looking," Guilliam roared, as he headed back through the laundry chutes, looking for her. "Make sure your guards are checking the garage floor. Check to see if any activity is going on down there."

"We're on it," one of the guys replied.

Guilliam added, "The rest of my team is on their way. Make sure you tell them where I am."

He and the guard with him quickly ran through every machine in the laundry area, looking for carts, looking for any hiding spots where Janelle could have been stashed. Anywhere. He turned a few minutes later to see Jasper and the rest of the team standing behind him. "She's gone," he muttered brokenly.

"She's not gone," Masters countered, stepping forward. "The asshole plucked her out of here, and that is bullshit, but you're not to blame."

"Thanks, but I am," he said, looking around. "Dear God, he could be anywhere with her by now."

"And he might be nowhere. Let's not lose hope right now. We need you to focus."

Guilliam nodded. "I'm focused, but you might have

trouble keeping me from killing this fucker when we find him."

"Understood, but that's not the problem right now," Masters noted.

"That's not the priority," Jasper added, "but nobody will give a shit if it's a clean deal, just don't put anybody in a bind."

Guilliam nodded again. "I know. And I know exactly how Mason felt when he popped Gabe. It's that twisted family. I need to get to the grandfather, and we need to call in the father and even the mother. I don't give a shit if she's taking chemotherapy or not," he snapped. "They will know where this guy is, and somebody will tell us."

With Masters at his side, he turned and raced back outside. Masters called him over to his vehicle.

"Come on. I'm driving. Tell me where we're going."

"First to the old folks' home," he muttered, "before that asshole calls me back."

"You think he will?"

"Oh, hell yes. And he'll make it bad, so I do what he needs me to do."

"You think he'll hurt her?"

He looked over at him and nodded. "Absolutely he will. At this point, I think they'll do whatever they need to, just to bring this to an end. And, for whatever reason, killing Mason is the end."

"That's an awful lot of hate," Masters said. "This whole thing has been one big long nightmare. To think that it's gotten this far makes me think it's declining."

"Maybe. The evil grandfather is probably dying, and this is his last wish. To see Mason dead. And maybe that's all there is to it. Maybe somebody is at the end of their line who just doesn't give a shit anymore."

He turned and nodded. "The grandfather?"

"It's certainly possible."

"Yeah, it is. The grandfather certainly had a bad reputation and, even as an old man now, might be angry enough to do something like this. And if he's an old codger who's been controlling the whims of everybody else in their lives for all these years, I can see that would be a serious problem."

Guilliam nodded. "As far as we know, the kidnapper is his only grandchild, Greg. So, the family dynasty dies with him."

"Wait, I thought this Greg guy was a cousin to Gabe."

"Yeah, the old man had two daughters. The one with cancer is the mother to Gabe. The other daughter is not the favorite, so she and Greg moved away years ago. So Greg is a blood relative in the grandfather's line."

"Okay, so if the kid Mason killed was the golden boy, that could make the grandfather really pissed off that Gabe was killed."

"Right, and, if the mother is dealing with cancer, she's quite likely to die soon too."

"So," Masters suggested, "from the grandfather's perspective, maybe he's thinking it's just losses upon losses, and the family line won't survive. Presumably it's all about the family surviving. It often is. You know that."

"I do know that," he agreed with a nod. "Even though sometimes I think a lot of these families shouldn't survive, their methodologies are archaic, and they're one step away from being feudal."

"Oh, they definitely are," Masters agreed, with a nod. "Maybe the added impetus is that the grandfather wants redemption for his dead grandson before granddaddy kicks the bucket."

As they pulled into the senior living facility, Guilliam started to hop out.

Masters grabbed his arm and said, "Buddy, you need to calm down."

"I'm calm," he bit off. "As calm as I will get until this bullshit is over. Janelle needs to be back where she belongs."

"And where is that?" Masters asked, a smile at the corners of his lips.

"You know exactly where that is," Guilliam snapped, with a hard glance in his direction.

"I do. Just checking to see if you had gotten there yet."

"Of course I did. I was there all along, which doesn't make it any easier. We've had a lot of years apart that didn't need to be, but I understood. I didn't like it, but I dealt with it. I won't deal with somebody stopping us now."

"Of course not," Masters agreed, "but we also can't go hog wild and give this guy the upper hand, so—"

"I know. I'm fine now. I'm completely calm," Guilliam stated.

"Like hell you are." Guilliam glared at him, and Masters just shrugged. "What, you think I can't tell?"

"Let's put it this way. I'm as calm as I'm likely to get," he snapped, as he turned and strode toward the front of the retirement home.

As he got there, the administrator of the home stood there, almost guarding the front door.

"You can't come in here," he stated.

"And who do you think is likely to stop me?" Guilliam asked, his voice silky soft.

"I already called for the police."

"That's good. I hope they bring the search warrants we

asked for."

"Search warrants?" he asked, paling visibly.

"Yes, search warrants. Those things that allow us to double-check all the criminal activity you're involved in."

"I'm not involved in any criminal activity," he protested.

"Yeah, so you say. Yet I highly doubt that will be the truth of it by the time we're done tearing apart your place." And look at that. The manager didn't even ask who they were or who they were after. The manager paled, and Guilliam nodded. "You're harboring a murderer, and I will talk to him whether you're okay with it or not."

"He hasn't left this place at all in years. No way he could have murdered anybody."

"Getting family members to do his dirty deeds and blackmailing others to do more dirty deeds does not exactly make him innocent," Guilliam snapped, as he glared at the man.

"Where are your cops?" he asked.

"It may take them a little bit longer to get all the search warrants ready. Meanwhile, move out of my way."

"He's an old man," he protested. "We've never had any trouble with him."

"Because he won't cause trouble here, since it won't get him anything. What he wants is revenge and retribution."

"Is that so wrong?" the other man asked. "He spent his whole life helping others."

At that, Guilliam stopped and stared at him.

The other man quickly backed up. "We don't know that he's done anything wrong," he protested. "And this needs to be tried in a court of law."

From a distance they heard somebody laughing, then shouting out to them. "Give it up, you old goat. Let them in to see me. I've got to have some entertainment in my life."

The other man groaned. "I could have just told them you were sleeping."

"Does it look like they give a shit if I'm sleeping? I'm pretty darn sure they would be all over us in two seconds anyway."

The manager glared at Guilliam. "You have no right to accost him."

"Accost him?" Guilliam repeated, frowning at him. "Now that I've seen your obvious allegiance to him, I am very interested in taking a deep dive into your life and history. We have five counts of murder already, and now it seems that you're an accomplice." With that said, Guilliam strode past the man, hearing him stutter and stammer.

Masters now spoke to the man, saying something along the lines of, "Just stay out of our way, but you'll need to collect whatever you want to bring with you because you'll be coming downtown with us."

The old man deeper inside cackled again. "You've got him good and scared now. Aren't you big tough boys? Have you come to arrest me?" he asked, with a sneer.

"Sounds like a great idea to me," Guilliam replied. "Not that you care. You don't care about much these days though, do you?"

"No, I sure don't. What's to care about? My whole family is gone because of assholes like you."

"Assholes like me?" Guilliam shook his head. "So, you kidnap an innocent young woman at her dead mother's bedside, so you can use her to get me to go kill somebody else, *huh*?"

The grandfather's expression was crafty. "Did it work?" he asked.

"No, it didn't."

"Ah, the poor woman, to think that she matters so little that you'll just let her die."

"Since when does killing one to kill another work?"

"In my world it works just fine," he said, with a smirk. "And if you think this is going in any other direction than the one I want, you're wrong. The only way we get out of this mess is if Mason dies. And I don't give a shit who dies with him."

CHAPTER 7

J ANELLE OPENED HER eyes, confused and disoriented. She
tried to shift, but she couldn't. She couldn't move at all.
She moaned softly as the pain kicked in. She couldn't even
tell where it was coming from. Was it her head or her body?
Everything hurt, everything ached, and yet why? She
desperately wanted to move, to roll to her side, or to maybe
get up somehow, and yet every movement she tried failed.
She was completely stuck.

And in the dark.

As her eyes adjusted, she noted she was tied up on the
floor of a van.

A man spoke beside her, followed by mocking laughter.

She didn't recognize the voice at first. As she slowly
shifted her gaze to the person speaking, she realized it was
the same guy, the fake doctor, and somehow she had been
moved. She was no longer in a laundry bin. "What did you
do to me?" she whispered, closing her eyes against the pain in
her head.

"Conked you on the head," he replied. "I didn't want to
deal with any more of your drama. That's the thing about
you women. You're so full of fucking drama."

She wasn't even sure what that meant and couldn't even

understand why he would hold that opinion. She was pretty sure that drama wasn't gender specific. "What do you want?" she muttered.

"From you? Nothing. You're staying right here, and, if you can keep yourself quiet, I won't have to club you on the head again," he shared, with a sneer. "That's what I want. I want cooperation."

"And yet I'm a prisoner," she whispered.

"You sure are, but apparently not the most brilliant prisoner, if you didn't already realize that when you first woke up. You are definitely a prisoner. You're not getting out anytime soon, and considering the fact that I'm not sure your boyfriend will cooperate," he explained, "you might just want to stay where you are and maybe sleep, so you don't have to see what's coming."

She wanted to scream and rail at him for doing this to her, but she knew that would just play into everything he liked about this activity. He was one of those assholes who thought he had the right to do anything he wanted, with no consequences. "He'll never kill Mason," she murmured.

"Too damn bad for you then, isn't it?" he asked, with a sour tone.

"I do know that—absolutely no way."

"Why? Doesn't he love you?"

"Because he's too honorable."

"What good is honor when you wake up in the middle of the night and discover that you're dead."

"If that were the case"—she opened her eyes and stared at him—"I wouldn't care, would I?"

"And you won't care soon anyway," he added, with a laugh. "Do you think I'm joking?"

"No, I don't think you're joking. I just think you're misguided. Guilliam isn't the kind of man who would kill someone to keep me alive."

"Oh, I wouldn't count on that. I saw the way he looked at you. He's the kind who will do anything to keep you from this fate."

"Maybe. But killing another person, especially a friend of his? That's just not happening."

He stopped for a moment, then asked, "Is Mason a friend of his?"

"Isn't Mason a friend of everybody? Unless you happen to be an asshole intent on hurting somebody in his family."

"I don't know what the deal was, but I don't give a shit. The old man is dying, and this is what's required to get his bloody fortune, so this is my deal."

"So, you don't care that an innocent man will die and that you're planning on killing me for the sake of your grandfather, a twisted and bitter old man?"

"God no, I don't care one little bit. Why would I? Do you think anybody cares about me?"

"No, probably not," she murmured. "Can't say I'm against seeing you locked up for the rest of your life either."

He gave a laugh. "Now that I can believe. The thing is, it won't matter because you won't see that because it's just not happening."

"You talk a big game," she noted, "but I'm not sure you have anything to back it up."

"Don't need anything to back it up," he stated. "But, if you keep talking, I'll make certain you suffer more than necessary when I do take you out."

She stared at him for a long moment. "Sure, you would. In fact, you would probably do this as a favor simply because you like to kill people. You don't care about people. You don't care about yourself. You don't care about your family. You just care about money. You're all about getting what you want and not giving a shit about what anybody else wants."

"Everybody else can fight for themselves," he said, his tone clipped. "And I don't give a crap what you say. Don't even bother psychoanalyzing me."

"Too late. You're so simplistic that you are one-dimensional," she said. "Money is your god. Anything else is secondary. You probably never had a decent relationship in your life."

He snorted at that.

"Or at least not with a woman who you didn't smack around and *tune up* all the time, somebody who would literally be a doormat for you because that's all you can handle."

"A doormat." He turned to glare at her.

"Somebody who doesn't have a strong-enough personality or enough self-esteem to stand up to you. Somebody who hasn't had the fear beat into her enough for you to keep up your façade of being a person they might even want. Of course they don't want you. Why would they?" she asked, with a headshake. "You're just—you're just another bully. Somebody determined to take what they want and not give a shit about right or wrong or what anybody else wants."

"Why should I give a shit about anybody else?" he asked, but a note of real curiosity filled his tone. "I don't understand that. Look at the world we live in. Why would I care about anybody else?"

She stared at him. "Do you really think it's that bad? That *all of it* is that bad?"

"Absolutely it's that bad," he declared, laughing. "Nobody else matters out there. It's just me, myself, and I."

"And where would you be if that's how your grandfather felt?"

"It *is* how my grandfather felt. It's how he still feels. Do you think he would be giving me a share of his wealth if I wasn't doing something for him? Everything in this world comes at a price, and for him to die knowing that the person he hates the most is also dead comes at a price."

Janelle continued. "What about your uncle? What about Gabe's father?"

"What about him? He lost everything in his life when he lost his son. He hasn't been the same since."

"Why? Because he realized he was responsible for raising a piece-of-shit son?"

"Whoa, not sure where you get that bravado from, but you better get rid of it real fast. I've got far better things to do than sit here and talk to you. And I sure won't sit here and let you bad-mouth my family."

She laughed, gritting through the pain that came with it. "Oh, so now it's your family? You didn't care about anything before, but suddenly now it's your family, and you care?"

He snorted. "I don't give a shit about anything, particularly you, so shut the fuck up."

She fell silent for the moment, knowing that he was unpredictable in this mood, but that aggression, that response, was enough to make her realize what a serious position she was in. There wouldn't be any talking this guy out of it. He was all about making sure that somebody paid the price so that he could keep his grandfather happy. "So, what if somebody paid you enough money for my life?" she asked in a conversational tone.

"They don't have enough money."

"You don't know that."

"Yeah, I do. My grandfather's got billions. That's tons of millions," he said, with a laugh.

"And what makes you think he'll leave it to you versus his own children? Doesn't it make more sense that he would leave it to them, the next generation?"

"They don't want it or need it," he said, with a dismissive gesture.

"Maybe, but family is family."

"And I am family, remember?"

"Sure, you are *part* of the family, but you're not the *next in line*, are you?"

"No," he muttered in a bored tone. "I'm not sure what you're trying to do, but you are way off the mark."

"Maybe. What about his favorite daughter?"

"What about her? She's busy dying from cancer."

She winced. "Wow, you don't have much compassion for anybody, do you."

"Not that bitch, I don't. Nope. You don't know what she's like. She even made her own son's life miserable. Gabe could never be good enough, could never stand up to be counted in any way that they saw him as a success. And when the news broke about his involvement in all the B&Es and why he went to Mason's place, supposedly to rape and torture his wife while Mason watched, it's as if she couldn't quite reconcile that with the baby boy she'd been grooming to be the best man possible."

"Maybe that grooming to be the best man possible ended up causing all of that."

"No doubt about it," he agreed, with a laugh. "And that may be why she got the cancer. Maybe it's the rotten side of her working its way out." He chuckled.

"Presumably she's your aunt, and you didn't have much to do with her."

"Nope, she doesn't have much to do with anybody who isn't part of her high-society life."

"I thought you were from that side of family," she noted, puzzled.

"Grandfather had two daughters. I belong to the second one," he explained.

"Ah, the least-favorite one."

He glared at her.

She shrugged. "You know it's true."

"I know it's true, but how do you know it?"

"Because that's how families work," she stated calmly. "There's always a favorite, and sometimes being the favorite doesn't necessarily get the favorite what they want. Plus, toward the end of the older couple's lives, they start to realize that maybe they should have done more for the other one."

"Yeah, they should have," he said, his voice harsh. "She didn't have it anywhere near as easy as my bloody aunt did."

"And you hate her for that too."

"Yeah, I do. No need to cut out my mother. No need to make her life so miserable that she ended up killing herself with drugs." He shook his head. "She had a trust fund, and she had me, but she didn't have anybody else. Sometimes you just need somebody else."

Janelle thought about that, thought about her own mother, and nodded. "I can't argue with that. I think we do need somebody else. I also think that sometimes what we need isn't necessarily what we think we need."

"Wow, isn't that philosophical," he quipped, with cutting mockery. "I get that you're just passing the time and maybe getting to know me, thinking I might change my mind," he noted in a laughing tone. "However, that won't work."

"I'm just trying to understand the family dynamic that brought all this on," she clarified. "Your mother died unloved, and now you're currying favor with your grandfather, bypassing your aunt and uncle, who you believe shouldn't have any claim to his fortune, particularly after your mother was treated so poorly."

"You're damn right," he muttered. "They shouldn't get anything."

"So, did you figure out how to blame them for all this? That would be a good strategy, a nice justice to see your aunt and uncle go to jail for all these murders."

He burst out laughing. This time his laughter was genuine. "Damn, why didn't I think of that? Shit, and here I thought you were just another dumb blonde."

"When I realized how much you hated them, it just made sense."

"Yeah, it makes a lot of fucking sense, but that doesn't mean I thought of it ahead of time, and now you're making me pissed off that I didn't."

He went silent at that point, and she could almost see the wheels churning around in his head, wondering if he could pull that off.

"Damn," he muttered. "Now I can't get that thought out of my mind." He cast her an odd look. "What the hell's wrong with you that you thought of something like that?"

"Hate is hate, right?" she replied. "When you hate somebody that much, and you don't think there will ever be any real justice for those who suffered so terribly, wouldn't you want to set them up for the fall?"

"Yeah, yeah," he muttered, warming to the idea.

"I guess it depends on whether they had anything to do with it or wanted no part of it."

"They wanted nothing to do with it," he muttered, with a wave of his hand. "They were far too good for it all. They wanted all of it to just go away, instead of seeking justice for their son."

"But that's because they knew what he did, right?"

"So what? He might have been stupid and shouldn't have been caught doing what he did, but that doesn't change anything."

"You don't think so?"

"No, of course not," he said, with a snort in her direction. "Don't go all Dr. Phil on me now."

"*Hmm.*" She stared at him. "What kind of attitude did they have toward their son at that point?"

"The two of them don't talk, and I'm pretty sure they blame each other for what happened to their son. She won't accept that's what Gabe did. Now dear old uncle accepts that part, but he's desperate to cover it up. And I thought it was all covered up until Granddad contacted me, and now he's one pissed-off old man, and you don't cross him."

"I gather that," she said, with a nod. "Then the question becomes, is it just him or, is anybody else involved in this nightmare?"

"No, it's just him, but you never really know when it comes to Grandpa. He could have another dozen people involved."

"So you didn't talk directly to your grandfather, just your uncle?" she asked, as she tried to figure out whether he was telling the truth, or it was just the truth as he knew it.

His gaze narrowed not answering the question, then asked suspiciously, "And what's it to you anyway?"

"There are always surprises in life." She just nodded and didn't dare say anything else to him because, as she well knew, people did people things, and not always for the clearest of reasons.

He gave a bark of laughter. "Too bad I have to kill you," he said. "You might be worth spending some time with."

"Yeah?" she asked, her heart sinking at the thought. "I would probably be too smart for you. Guys like you, you always want bimbos with brains, but brains they don't use."

He nodded. "That's not a bad way to look at it. Bimbos with brains they don't use. That's implying that they know what to do with them."

"Yeah, but you're the guy who thinks women don't know anything."

"Oh, some of them do," he agreed. "I had a couple nice girlfriends for a while, but revenge does tend to make you a little angry."

She frowned at that. "Revenge, *huh*?"

"Yeah, revenge."

"Did you ever take out your need for revenge on your aunt and uncle?"

"No, not yet, but you're making me think I need to."

"Particularly in case something goes wrong in your world now. I mean, what will you do if you're the one holding the bag on this, and they walk away scot-free?"

"But they aren't involved," he pointed out, "so your theory doesn't hold."

She wasn't exactly sure that she even had a theory at this point. She was just tossing out anything to make him stop and think, something to make him reassess this game he was playing with her life. She knew he was somebody who just didn't give a shit. But she did, and anything she could do to make her world function without all this killing would be lovely. "What if you don't get any of your grandfather's money?"

He jerked his head in her direction. "Don't say that again or you'll regret it."

She waited a little bit longer and then added, "If my son was killed, I don't think I would check out quite so easily."

"What are you saying?" He looked over at her suspiciously.

She shrugged. "If my son was killed, and I wanted true justice to happen, I wouldn't just give up, like your aunt did."

"Yeah? Well, she did. In case you've forgotten, she's also fighting for her life with cancer."

"Right, and that could change things. I don't know whether it makes it worse though, or better."

"What do you mean?" he snapped, getting up and walking over, crouching in the van to talk to her.

She frowned, as he navigated around commercial laundry bags, the kind they would use at hospitals. In fact she was tucked into a laundry bag. "I don't suppose you want to loosen the ties on my hands a little bit. Could you? I know I'm supposed to be a model prisoner, but I can't feel my fingers and toes. A little circulation would help a lot." He glared at her, and she nodded. "It's not as if I can try anything. I've got no place to go anyway."

"That's true," he muttered. He pulled down the laundry bag that had been tied around her neck, then quickly loosened the bonds on her wrists.

With her hands loose, she slowly rubbed them together, almost crying out with the pain at the movement. "Damn," she muttered. "How could something like that hurt so much?"

"Circulation is everything," he said, without looking at her too much.

"Right, got it. Okay, thank you."

He didn't say anything. Was he waiting for her to put her hands back inside the damn bag again? She hoped not and was rather desperate to have her hands free. She waited for him to say something, but, when he didn't, she just relaxed ever-so-slightly, whispering, "It's amazing what pins and needles feel like."

"Yep. My uncle James, he was a bit of a bastard that way. Him and that punk-ass son of his, Gabe, used to tie me up just for fun, whenever we went over to visit. Not that my uncle was ever partaking in it, but he's the one who showed Gabe how to do it. He always left me strung up for a while, until somebody would come looking for me. I hated that asshole."

"So why are you doing anything to avenge Gabe's death?"

"I'm not," he declared, frowning at her. "I don't give a shit about him. I'm perfectly happy that he's gone. Besides, it's one less for me to share the estate with."

"Right. So, for you, it's literally all about the money."

"Exactly, all about the money," he repeated, with that mocking tone. "I did say that earlier," he pointed out, "but, once again, people just don't listen."

"I listened," she corrected. "I just wasn't sure that could be your strongest motive."

"And why the hell not?" he asked, staring at her. "I don't have any hidden motives here."

"No, but maybe you're also happy that cousin of yours is gone. Hell, maybe you even did something to make sure."

He snorted at that. "If I'd thought about it, I might have. If I'd realized he would cause so much trouble for me, I might have. As it is, that Mason guy took care of it."

She nodded. "Yet now Mason is to pay the price for getting rid of Gabe."

"Yep. The ultimate price. And I think I'm supposed to take care of his wife at the same time."

"But you expect somebody else to do the killing?"

"Sure. And it would be nice if it worked out that way. Then I don't have to get involved. It seems like every time I get involved, it gets a little harder to get out of that grasp," he noted. "The more killing you get involved in, it does get easier—the killing part, that is. Sometimes it's damn hard to get out without leaving evidence behind. Yet the more I kill, Grandpa just wants me to kill more."

"So, *you* did all those killings?" she asked.

"All what killings?" he asked cagily.

She thought about what Guilliam had shared with her. "I heard there have been a lot of killings, like five or six people who failed to kill Mason or to protect the boss man behind it."

Her kidnapper shrugged. "Probably a lot more than that, which is also why I'm making damn sure that my grandfather is leaving me his estate. I'm not doing these killings for nothing. He may have taught me how to kill, but man, that guy, that old geezer, is brutal. He was my instructor when it came to this shit, but he can't hold a rifle steady anymore, so I'm expected to finish this off, so he can die in peace."

She winced. "Any idea how many he's killed?"

"In his lifetime? Who knows. Dozens for sure," he said, with another dismissive wave of his hand. "Anybody who resisted him was killed. Listen to any of the tales about some of the locals who tried to argue with him, who fought him on some issue, or who tried to raise a group against him, and you can bet that Grandpa's the one who popped them and buried them out in the desert somewhere." Her kidnapper chuckled. "Just go to the history books and look up missing persons. It'll be due to him."

"Nobody said anything? Nobody did anything?" she asked in shock.

"Who would stop him?" He laughed. "He's a law unto himself and has been for a very long time. Nobody ever expects an old man to do something like that. I know that my uncle was suspected of doing a lot of it there for a while, but it was never Uncle James. It was the old guy that whole time."

"And you," she pointed out.

"Yeah, and me," he added, with a shrug. "But it's not what I wanted do. It's what I had to do."

"Right," she muttered, trying to keep the sarcasm out of her tone. But it was obvious from his sharp look that she hadn't succeeded. "You're correct. That was sarcastic. It's just hard to imagine how many deaths he got away with all these years."

"Remember that people always go missing," he noted. "Just because you don't know who they are or where they went missing from doesn't mean that the same person was killing them."

"I just can't imagine," she whispered. "So many families destroyed, and all because of what?"

"Because they crossed him," he stated.

"And that's the life you want for yourself?"

"No, the world is changing. Hell, it changed long before he ever stopped. If he hadn't had that stroke a good ten years ago, there would have been a hell of a lot more killings."

"And given the change in the times, with new technology and potentially a new chief of police, he might not have gotten away with any of it," she pointed out.

"That's true enough. I'm pretty damn sure the chief of police has his number, but she doesn't have any proof."

"She's probably getting that now. People are sniffing around, looking to take down somebody like that. So you can bet all the evidence will start coming out of the woodwork."

"Not for Grandfather," he stated confidently. "He's bought everybody off."

"Everybody?"

"Except for that one, the chief of police," he admitted. "And the fact that it's a woman just pisses him off even more."

"Of course. But then he spent his lifetime keeping women down, where I'm sure he thought they belonged. An interesting position for the father of two daughters."

He burst out laughing at that. "You're damn right. That is where they belong."

"Of course that would be your attitude." He glared at her, but Janelle just shrugged. "Think about it."

Just then his phone buzzed. He looked down at it and smiled. "Look at that. Your little friend contacted my family." She frowned at him, while he nodded. "Now this shit's fixing to get fun."

"Why is that?" she asked, as she thought about the implications.

"Because my grandfather, he won't give an inch. He'll probably tell your boyfriend quite cheerfully what he's doing and what he's done, but no way in hell will he let your buddy off the hook. Mason will die, … or you will," he declared, with a hard look her way. "Believe me that me and my grandfather, we don't give a shit which one."

THE COPS WERE behind Guilliam and Masters, having arrived at the retirement home soon after they did, but the old man was still just grinning like a fool. He wasn't prepared to talk or to otherwise help them out in any way.

"And your son-in-law?" Guilliam asked. "Does he know this is what you're up to?"

He snorted. "That son-in-law of mine is nothing but a coward at this point. Losing his boy, that just ruined him. He went soft and has been useless to me ever since."

"A death like that has a tendency to affect people," Guilliam stated, with a gaze at the old man who showed no signs of softening.

"No time for that shit. You make good on what you need to do, and then you move on."

"Right. So, he was supposed to grieve for a moment, then get back in the saddle, is that it?"

"That's what I just said, isn't it?" he barked. He shook his head. "You're as stupid as the rest of them."

"And that's how you got through life, isn't it? Insulting people, badgering people, probably killing people too."

The old guy laughed. "You don't know the half of it." He sneered. "Death is cheap."

"Not to the rest of the people in the family."

"Who gives a shit? Women, they just turn around and find another guy. It's not like they give a shit. It's all temporary anyway."

"Is that how you felt about your wife?"

He turned and glared. "You don't get to talk about my wife. She was an angel."

"If she put up with you, she must have been," Guilliam replied.

"I don't care what you've got to say to me," he snapped, glaring at everybody. "I'll be dead before I ever hit jail anyway."

"But at least you've admitted to it."

"I would admit to a whole lot more," he added, "but I will wait until I know for sure that Mason is dead." He smiled. "That's what I care about."

"Because he shot your grandson in a home invasion. A home invasion where Gabe targeted Mason's wife."

"Exactly. And that stupid grandson of mine shouldn't have done it, yet he didn't deserve death."

"What about all these people you've killed or had killed? Did they deserve death?"

"You bet they did," he declared. Then the old man got crafty. "Bring me proof of Mason's death, and I'll help you clear up dozens of old cases."

With that, the chief of police walked past and glared at him.

"Yeah, yeah, yeah. Get that set of boobs away from me," he muttered. "You shouldn't even be in that job."

"Good to know I have your support," Alex said, beaming a smile in his direction, just making him glare even more. "And just because you say so doesn't make things the way you want."

"It should. Women don't belong in law enforcement."

"I'm not sure assholes like you belong on earth either," she added, with that same cheerful smile. "So, I guess we'll both be disappointed. All you've done is cause chaos and mayhem all around you." She glanced around at the senior care home. "How many other people in here have you coerced into doing your bidding?"

He shrugged. "I didn't do anything I don't always do. People are generally quite happy to give me what I need."

"Yeah, and why is that? Do you threaten to rape their daughters and to kill their sons?"

He glared at her. "No, I don't have to. Not anymore. Once you make a name for yourself and raise a little hell, everybody's petrified of you, and that's the way you work it. Then it doesn't matter. By the time anybody thinks about resistance, the thought has already left their heads, and their resistance has got up and gone." He laughed. "Fear is a huge motivator."

She stared at him and nodded. "It is a huge motivator, but your grandson Gabe was still a useless piece of shit."

He struggled to get up out of his chair, wheezing in fury.

She added, "And you knew it, but still, all you did was cause hellishness for everybody else. What have we got, five, six dead people, all because you coerced them into this Gabe mess?" She shook her head. "Who killed them all off? That's what I want to know. Who killed them all? We know it wasn't you."

"None of your business." He glared at her. "You all think you know everything, but you know nothing. It's not just me affected by my grandson's death," he muttered.

She stared at him for a long moment, then turned to Guilliam. "Have you had any chance to get an idea where she is?"

"No. This asshole's not giving in."

The old coot laughed. "I might be inclined to do something to save her, but you know my condition. I want Mason dead."

"Oh, I heard you, and you're not getting that."

"Yeah, says you. It's very simple. If you don't do the job, she dies. And the person who kidnapped her will kill Mason anyway. I was just keeping him out of jail a little bit longer."

"A little bit longer?" Guilliam repeated. "Meaning, you expect he'll end up there anyway?"

"Most certainly, particularly after I'm gone. It's always been me who kept him in check."

"Are we talking about the one doing all your bidding? You probably corrupted him yourself."

Just then another set of police cars arrived, and the old man was slowly moved to be loaded into a car, to be taken to the jail.

The old man laughed. "It's not like I will talk to you, *Chief of Police*, down there, any more than I'm doing here."

She smiled. "Maybe not, but you can't terrorize anybody else, and now we can talk to your family and other minions without your interference, with the assurance that you'll never be back."

He glared at her. "Yeah, well, they better not say anything fucking wrong about me. I'm the reason they had it so good all these years."

"*Right*," she muttered, her tone dry and caustic. "Like absolutely nobody else in this world is any good, just you, correct?"

He glared at her.

She returned her own warning gaze. "Remember that it's *my* jail you're going to. So, I highly suggest you think very hard about what you have to say next."

He continued to glare at her and shut up.

She nodded. "Good choice." She looked over at the manager. "Sir, you will also be needed down at the station."

"I can't leave here."

"The owners have already been contacted," she noted. "They're coming in for questioning as well, due to suspicious activity in their facility. I believe they have something to say to you."

"They know perfectly well everything I've been doing," he declared stiffly. "I've devoted my life to those people."

"Good, then you'll be quite happy to tell us all about it."

He flushed and shook his head. "Not if you treat me badly."

"Why do you think I will treat you badly?" she asked curiously, looking at him. "You think I will put you on the rack and stretch you out or something? Use all those old medieval methods?"

He glared at her. "It's not nice of you to tease me either. I've never been arrested before."

"That's all right. You will soon get arrested and have that experience," she explained. "With any luck you'll spend the rest of your life in jail, and you won't ever get arrested again."

He stared at her in shock. "I won't go to jail for anything. I didn't do anything wrong."

"That remains to be seen," she stated. "When you're involved with someone who commits these violent crimes, you are also guilty by association."

"No, no, no, no, no, no," he whined. "He's the one who arranged everything."

"Yeah, we know," she agreed, as she motioned to the two officers nearby, who each took an arm and directed the manager outside. "And you let him, even helped him. Aiding and abetting is what it's called," she pointed out, as she pushed his head down to keep him from hitting it as he got into the black-and-white. "We will talk more down at the station." And, with that, she slapped the top of the cruiser and ordered, "Get him into a cell as soon as you can."

Then she turned to another manager, who had been brought on to replace him. She looked at the woman and asked, "What's your name?"

"Elsey Howitch," replied the woman nervously.

Guilliam walked up and asked, "Well, Elsey, what can you tell us about this place?"

She looked from one to the other and said, "I don't know what you mean."

"You need to think carefully about what you say next," Guilliam warned, "because we already know the old man is involved in at least five murders."

She squeaked out an astonished cry.

He nodded. "We're pretty sure the real number is way-the-hell higher. But in this last few weeks or so, we've counted that many."

"Oh my God, oh my God," she cried out.

"So, now I need to know just how much you helped him."

The woman fell apart right in front of them.

"I didn't want to. I didn't want to at all," she wailed.

"And what is it you didn't want to do?"

"I had to go shopping for him all the time. I had to pick up stuff, like phones and things. I don't … I don't even know sometimes what I picked up. I just had to go pick up deliveries, things in boxes."

"What do you mean, had to?" the chief of police asked, her tone hard.

Elsey turned, and her hands shook as she wrung them in front of her. "It was either that or lose my job."

"And who told you that?"

"The manager. He told me that I had to."

"And yet you're a manager yourself."

She nodded. "But he's the boss, and I have to do what he says, or I don't have a job, and, if I don't have a job, I can't feed my family."

Guilliam studied her. Seeing the truth in her gaze, he turned to the chief of police and said, "This is a waste of my time."

"Maybe," she agreed, with a shrug. The chief of police turned to question Elsey. "Do you ever see his grandson?"

"Yes, yes, he comes here often," she replied eagerly, as if happy to answer something.

"Did you ever hear what they talked about?"

She winced. "They always shut up when people walk in. It's always hush-hush secret stuff," she said, "but it's always bad stuff. He's no good. That man, he's no good."

"Which one?" he asked.

She whispered, "The grandson. That one, he's no good."

"Oh, I got it," Guilliam agreed. "We also believe he kidnapped a young woman today."

She stared at him and nodded. "I did hear something," she murmured. "I don't know though. … I don't know if it's relevant." Her gaze went from one to the other. "They mentioned something about Mason." She looked hopeful that the information would be of use.

Guilliam nodded. "Yes, they've kidnapped a young woman in order to get someone to kill this Mason person."

"To kill?" she asked, paling. "I thought I just heard them say *shot*."

"Yes, you did. He was shot, and he's in the hospital. But they failed to kill him the first time around, so they're trying for a second attempt."

"Oh dear, oh dear," she muttered, almost sobbing now. "I had nothing to do with it. Please, you must believe me. I had nothing at all to do with it."

He believed her, and he could tell from the chief of police's face that she did too. "What else did you hear?" he asked.

She thought hard. "It was always just talk." And then she frowned. "It was strange today, as he was talking about things he doesn't deal with."

"Like what?"

"Like laundry."

At that, Guilliam nodded. "We suspect that the kidnapped woman was taken out in one of those wheeled laundry carts."

She clapped her hands to her face. "Oh my gosh, that poor woman." She looked from one to the other. "Why? Why her?"

Guilliam barked a harsh laugh. "Because he wants me to kill Mason, and she is my partner. They've told me that, if I don't kill Mason, they will kill her."

That left the other woman in tears, as she stared at him, shaking her head back and forth. "I didn't know. I didn't know."

"Maybe not," he conceded, studying her closely. "However, if you know anything else, anything at all, this is the time to tell us, before we find out on our own and realize that you're withholding information."

"No, no, no. I don't know anything. It's just little bits that I might have heard. It's always hard with him because he talks and then shuts up, so you don't know. You're not supposed to hear anything, and over time you just block it all out. You ignore it because he's that kind of a man."

"Oh, I hear you," Guilliam noted, "but, if you heard anything today, you need to tell us now."

Another voice called out, "I heard the same thing she did."

He turned to see an old lady in a wheelchair off to the side.

"He used to brag about all his escapades," she began, her voice sad. "I thought he was a good man at first, but he hadn't been here very long when I heard him bullying the staff. I told him to leave the staff alone, that he didn't need to be making them miserable. He told me to shut up, and, if I didn't, he would make sure that somebody in my family paid for it." She looked over at them. "Please, don't ever let that man come back here again."

The chief of police approached her and nodded. "We'll make sure that doesn't happen, but we will need proof of what he's been up to."

"Didn't he confess?"

"He did, but, if he recants, then I'm left with not a whole lot to make a case from. So I need evidence."

"Of course. I do know that he's always talking with that grandson of his, and as Elsey told you, they were always talking about what they would do if they needed to."

"And did you hear what they said today?"

"Something about a laundry cart and a laundry van."

Guilliam was already pulling out his phone. "That makes sense. I presume that my team is already on it."

"He said it wouldn't look … I remember them saying something about it wouldn't look like a laundry van."

"And yet it would be," Guilliam added.

"Right." She nodded. "I hope you get that woman back. And I hope that asshole never gets loose again." She stopped as she was about to wheel away. "One time he did talk about using murder to keep people in line. I thought he was joking at first because he had just arrived, so I didn't know him well enough. But now I don't think he was joking at all."

Guilliam nodded. "No, I don't think he was joking. We've been told that is how he controlled people. We've even heard rumors that, way back when, he would pick out a few people, have them disappear, all as a lesson for everybody else."

She winced. "Somebody here mentioned that he had a hand in her son going missing years ago, and that, if she could afford to be anywhere else, she definitely wouldn't be here."

Guilliam frowned at that. "Are you sure? Because this old man could afford to be somewhere else or even at home with private care, so I'm not even sure why he's here."

"He likes the location," she said in a dry tone. "And the fact that he can bully everybody."

The chief of police added, "He could probably go to a more expensive place, but he has his local connections, and I presume they treat him the way he wants to be treated."

"Ah"—Guilliam nodded—"that would explain it. And who's this woman?"

The woman in the wheelchair replied, "She's here. You could probably talk to her. I know she's traumatized. She hasn't been here very long, and, when she realized he was here, … she's, well, she's not been the same ever since."

"Of course not." Guilliam sighed. "When you start a reign of terror, it doesn't end just because someone wants it to end."

"I don't think he wanted it to end at all," the woman stated. "I think he's been more than happy to make sure everybody feared him and did exactly what he told them to do."

"And did you overhear anything else he may have said, especially today?" Guilliam asked, as the chief of police took off to find the other woman.

"I don't know. I really don't know. I thought so many of the stories were hogwash, until I realized he was serious, and then I basically stayed as far away from him as I could. I locked myself in my room a couple times just to avoid him." When Guilliam frowned, she winced. "That old man is still *randy*, and I wasn't interested. He kept making suggestions that he thought would interest me."

"Good Lord," Guilliam muttered. The old man might have been in his eighties. The woman in front of him was regal and had to be well into her seventies. More power to her if she wanted a relationship, but to think that this guy would be threatening women of her age just meant the old coot was clueless as to what women wanted. "How pathetic it is that he would force that type of relationship on women."

"It's the only way he could ever have any relationship," she stated, with half a smile. "Nobody liked him. Everybody hated him in fact, and, if they didn't hate him, they were terrified of him. It just took me a little bit longer than the others to find out. I'm not from this area originally. So, when I moved here, I had no idea we had a serial killer at this retirement home, let alone one who has gone unpunished all these years."

"Have you met any of his family?" Guilliam asked.

"I have. The daughter was here a couple times. A very

intense woman," she noted. "I'm not sure that I particularly would have been friends with her either. There was talk of her coming to live here later in life, but I gather that her surgeries and cancer treatment may not be going all that well. I got the impression that since the grandson died, the old coot's been worse than he used to be and very uncaring about anybody but himself. He would often bring his daughter to tears."

"Did you ever have any idea if she was involved in any of it?"

"I don't know. One time I interrupted an argument between them, and she was very upset about the death of her son. The old man yelled at her, saying that her son was a useless piece of shit or something along that line," she said, with a wave of her hand. "But then he tended to say that about anybody he didn't like in the moment."

"Of course," Guilliam noted. "And, with all his family members being equally dysfunctional, I can't imagine that the grandson who died would have been any different from the others."

"I don't even know what happened, but they blame somebody named Mason."

"The grandson was involved in a series of B&E crimes, and at one point he targeted one of Mason's friends. Law enforcement was having a problem getting the victims to come forward, presumably out of fear of retribution. So Mason made some public statements, hoping to get him to break into his home, so they could get an opportunity to send him to jail. Mason's wife was supposed to be away that weekend, but, at the last minute, she decided to spend the weekend home with Mason. So, when the grandson arrived and broke into Mason's house, he was delighted to find her there and decided that he would torment and rape her in front of Mason. That didn't go so well for him."

The woman stared at him in shock, and Guilliam nodded.

"Mason ended up shooting and killing him, obviously in defense of his wife."

"Thank God for that," she muttered in horror.

"Exactly. The family chose to proclaim that the intruder was innocent, with absolutely no idea why he was even there at the time. They blamed Mason for it."

"So now they're trying to kill him?" she cried out in shock.

"Yes, although that B&E happened years ago. Yet Mason was shot a few weeks ago and is recovering in the hospital," Guilliam explained. "He is under guard, of course, but we're very aware that somebody is still attempting to take him out."

"And did I hear something about an attempt to coerce you into doing that?" she asked cautiously.

"That's what the old coot's hoping for. He figures that, by kidnapping my girlfriend, he could apply enough pressure to make me go kill Mason."

She shook her head.

He smiled at her. "Obviously that's not happening."

She grimaced. "Yet your poor girlfriend …"

"Yes. I'm not sure who has her, but it appears the other grandson is involved."

"He's no good either," she declared. "The grandson orders around everybody here like they're his servants and expects them to wait on him hand and foot." She shook her head. "That whole family is messed up."

"Yes."

At that, the chief of police returned with an older woman. They quickly questioned her, and she confirmed the same thing.

"Now, the question is, where would the grandson hold his kidnap victim?"

"I don't know why he would take her anywhere," replied the first lady in the wheelchair. "If he's making sure that you kill somebody in the hospital, wouldn't he stay at the hospital to see the job done?"

A slow smile dawning on his face, Guilliam held up one finger. "I'll be back in a second." He quickly bolted outside. He got Jasper on the phone and asked, "Where are you?"

"I'm in Mason's room right now."

"Okay, there's a good chance that this asshole is somewhere close by. I don't know why I didn't think of it myself, but I'm putting it down to stress and circumstances," he admitted, with a groan. "What if he's parked right in the hospital parking lot, waiting to see if I show up to take care of Mason?"

"You think he would do that?" Jasper asked doubtfully.

"What I think is that this guy can't afford any mistakes. I don't know why he's doing this at all, outside of the fact that his grandfather wants him to. I don't know what kind of pressure is involved in getting him to do it, if there even is any. For all I know he's quite happy to do all this, but the grandfather will want proof, at the very least to know that I'm there. And the only way is for the grandson to be close at hand to see me walk inside."

"Okay, I'll mobilize the troops, and we'll do a full search outside," Jasper replied.

"You need to do it discreetly," Guilliam said.

"I do know how to do my job," Jasper noted.

"I get it, but …"

"I know. I understand. Right now it's all about Janelle. Are you done there?"

"Yeah. The chief of police is here and she'll get statements from everybody."

"Good enough," Jasper said, ending the call.

MOVING QUICKLY, GUILLIAM headed toward the hospital parking lot. He knew that the outside search would have gone on at the same time as the inside, but, if they didn't find anything, the kidnapper would be thinking he was safe. That was good. Guilliam wanted him to feel like he was safe. Guilliam wanted him to believe that everything was going his way. The kidnapper was wrong, of course, but that would give him a sense of security.

As Guilliam pulled into the rear hospital parking lot, he deliberately got out, walked around, checked to make sure he was visible, then strode around the hospital, heading for the front of the building. He felt eyes on him, and that was important. Everybody needed to know that he was supposedly there to do a job—finishing off Mason. No way in hell Guilliam would, and he knew that his team all knew that, but this asshole was counting on Janelle's kidnapping to be enough of a pressure point for him.

Honestly, all this made him nervous. If anything happened to Janelle, he wasn't sure what he would do. He found it unbelievable that it had come to this. After everything the *get revenge on Mason* group had been working on, to think that somebody just walked in and snatched Janelle in the hospital—sitting there with the body of her mother, spending a few minutes before they took the body away—was just obnoxious. And that's what these people worked on. They utilized pain and fear, making people suffer as much as they could. He hoped this asshole was somebody Guilliam would meet personally, like with his fists, making him suffer a little for what he was putting Janelle through.

As he thought about the old man in the retirement home and all the power he once wielded, Guilliam couldn't imagine what the old bastard had probably gotten away with. Guilliam hoped he and his team and the local authorities could get names and dates of the missing at least, so they could close some cases and could offer some family members a bit of solace in finally hearing the truth about what happened to their loved ones.

Revealing the truth was a double-edged sword, since it would also hurt people to know what happened and to realize how much this asshole and his family had destroyed with their disregard for human life. And yet people like that were always living among us. Yet it seemed as if, in these modern-day times, those people weren't so readily getting away with their crimes. This old guy had perfected his system though. He'd perfected his method of haunting people. He knew what buttons to push and how hard to push them.

Guilliam had been on base and also had been overseas, even back when the old man had been killing, blackmailing, threatening, abusing others in the Coronado area. A decade ago the old man had relocated his terrorism tactics to the senior care home, which still was a mystery to unfold. When Guilliam's phone buzzed, he finally got the file he'd request- ed on the second grandson. As he went through the rap sheet, he shook his head. "Another fucking asshole," he muttered.

This grandfather absolutely loved these screwed-up grandsons. Guilliam wondered what part the fathers to these two men had played in all this. Were the two fathers of the same bent? And, if so, why weren't those two fathers getting involved here? Yes, Guilliam had heard how the father of Gabe—the one stupid enough to break into Mason's home and to threaten harm to Tesla—had checked out of life, especially with his wife now dying of cancer. And with the other father to the other son out of the picture, the grandfather now seemed to lean on his remaining grandson to carry out his vile acts for him.

Guilliam wondered just how much the grandfather's wishes were catered to here. How much did he terrorize his own family when they didn't follow suit? When they didn't do whatever the old coot required of them? Had they been given the same kind of treatment as these townspeople? Guilliam believed they did because, once an asshole, always an asshole. Still, Guilliam couldn't imagine growing up to learn that level of disregard for human life.

It did explain the kid Mason had killed. Gabe probably was bored, even emulating his grandfather, all to potentially earn his favor, to inherit the grandfather's wealth, skipping over his parents and going straight for the next generation. Guilliam had seen it before. If these dysfunctional families couldn't get love from their blood relatives, they would get it from another individual. If money was also involved, all the better.

Guilliam paused at that, wondering just how much money the grandfather might control. He quickly sent a text to Jasper, asking him for information on the old man's combined estate and who might be in the will.

When Jasper phoned him a little later, he asked, "Are you still outside?"

"I am," Guilliam replied. "Why?"

"Just confirming. We're checking the license plates on every van out there," he explained. "We can't imagine it would be any other vehicle, but we don't want to take that chance."

"Of course not," he murmured. "And I agree. I doubt it will be any other vehicle just because he'll still have to hide her. And the old man's net worth?"

"It used to be an incredible amount of money, but it's much less now. Some of the CEO father's business decisions didn't go over so well, and he lost the company quite a bit of money over recent years. The grandfather has very little respect for him or for his daughter for marrying him, especially after he managed to deplete their resources so badly."

"Right. So, the old guy probably hoped that his grand-kids would step up and be what he wanted them to be."

"Quite likely," Jasper agreed. "And it did appear that both grandkids, the grandsons, attempted to step up. In each case only one child came from each of the two daughters. I think one daughter passed already, and the one remaining daughter has breast cancer."

"Do we know if she's doing okay with the cancer, maybe fighting it off, or if she in palliative care right now?"

"Good question. I'll see if I can find out."

Guilliam rang off and returned to his search of the parking lot, quiet, unobtrusive, just walking through, trying to be visible, yet not in a threatening way. What he really wanted was for the kidnapping asshole to see him, to see that he was here, to see that he wanted to find Janelle, alive and in good shape—maybe concerned enough for her to consider finishing off Mason.

That might not be the message Guilliam should be sending, but he would do a lot right now to stop this asshole from doing anything stupid. And when it came to stupid, already so many incidents had been so stupid that it seemed to be the proper word here. Making a very visible entrance through the rear door, he headed inside the hospital. As soon as he made it just inside, he settled into a spot where he could watch the outside world. Would the kidnapper expect Guilliam to come back out again in a hurry or something else? How would the kidnapper know if the job had been completed? That was the real trick. How to find that out.

Talking to Jasper on the phone again, Guilliam said, "I think it's been long enough."

Jasper snorted. "For you, yeah, but, for any other assassin, a real assassin, you know perfectly well that they would still be assessing the place."

"And yet, as far as this grandson is concerned, he thinks he can coerce me into killing Mason. He also knows that I have the skills to do that. Then the question becomes, how does he find out that Mason is gone?"

"Most likely from someone in the hospital, who he coerced to notify him, due to blackmail, physical threats, whatever. Let's not forget all the military people they've already had involved in Mason's sniper attempt."

Guilliam suggested, "We should ask the old coot about that."

Jasper agreed. "That's a damn good point."

"Contact the chief of police, will you? I'm pretty sure the grandfather has some connections on base, even within the police department, that he's probably hoping nobody finds out about. Didn't someone say that dear old grandpa may have served in the military and how that really ticked off the dead grandson?"

"Oh, we'll find out all right," Jasper stated, "and if the old coot puts any more of us in danger, we'll have his ass in a court-martial."

"Yeah, well, I hope we just throw him in the brig and leave him there." Guilliam snorted.

"Meanwhile," Jasper shared, "we have things in place inside the hospital. A Code Blue will be announced at any moment, and a crash cart is on the way to Mason's room. We'll keep Mason's room secured. Plus, some of our volunteers are manning the phone system, as well as the nurses' stations on the first floor and on Mason's floor. That way our story should be consistent. So, once you hear the code, then leave after a minute or so."

"Will do. I'll talk to you in a few minutes." And shortly thereafter, he quickly walked outside, making sure to glance nervously around, and then smoothly moved toward his vehicle—as if the job were done, and it was time to get lost. Once in his vehicle, he deliberately drove past the public entrances and headed out of the back parking lot.

Once out of sight of anyone in the hospital parking lot, he made several quick turns, then parked in a used car lot, not very far away. Now on foot, he doubled back into the hospital through a side entrance for Employees Only. He sent a text to Jasper. **Back inside, avoiding cameras. I'll wait and see what happens.**

Jasper sent a thumbs-up. **Interrogation of old man and manager is underway. Looks like the manager is interested in talking.**

Good. The old bastard will probably happily tell us

everything he did, which I suspect is quite a bit. It's the only way he'll get out of this without heavy prison time, though it's hard to say how much he's involved in it personally—or how long he'll live.

He's involved. And we know he's all about saving his own ass, even to the point of throwing his one remaining grandson under the bus.

With his phone on vibrate, Guilliam sat quietly in a dark corner, near the reception desk, watching as people came and went through the main entrance. When no sign of anything came from the front, he motioned to the nearby security guard, who gave him a headshake. Guilliam nodded in return, and just then a phone call came through the main switchboard in the lobby. They all waited and listened, as the switchboard operator answered as coached.

"Yes, we do have a Mason Callister here," she replied, then hesitated. "I'm sorry to tell you that he didn't make it." The woman manning the phones turned toward the security guard, who nodded back at her while moving closer. "Yes. I'm afraid he's just passed away." And, with that, the operator ended the call.

The nurse seated beside her frowned. "I don't like doing that," she whispered to her temporary coworker, "as we have no way of knowing who that even was on the phone."

The woman who worked for Jasper just smiled at the nurse. "The good news is, if we don't know who called, then chances are, he also doesn't know what we're up to."

The nurse shrugged. "As long as his wife doesn't hear the news."

"Oh, you mean, the news that her husband has passed away? That is not likely, since she is in the hospital room with him right now."

"I know, I know. I just … I don't normally do this kind

of stuff."

"Good," the woman stated, with a smile. "I'll be at this post for a while. Once you are on the phones again, if anybody calls to ask about Mason, you give them the same message."

"And what if it's somebody else?" she asked. "What if it's a family member?"

"There will be a public announcement once this is all over with," the woman reassured her. "This is just for the moment. Remember that a woman has been kidnapped, and her life is at stake, not to mention Mason's."

The nurse pinched her lips together and nodded. "I remember that, but I hope you catch this asshole soon."

"Oh, we will," the woman declared, with quiet certainty. "We will."

With that, Guilliam turned and slipped back out of the hospital.

CHAPTER 8

J ANELLE ROLLED STIFFLY inside the laundry bag, trying to make herself more comfortable.

Her kidnapper glared over at her. "Don't try any funny stuff."

She glared right back at him. "I'm sore and I'm stiff," she snapped. "What do you expect me to do?"

"Lie still," he barked. His gaze flew to the blacked-out window to study what was going on around them. He'd already made two phone calls, asking the same question, and he'd been laughing ever since. Now he studied the activity in the parking lot. Then he stilled and whispered, "Well, I'll be. There he is."

She groaned, trying not to think about what might have transpired.

"Who would have thought a bitch like you would be worth it, after all?" he asked, followed by more laughter. "Granddad will be damn happy."

When he turned on the engine, she spoke up. "Wait, wait. You said, if he did it, you would let me go."

He turned and gave her a sneer. "Why the hell would I let you go?" he asked. "You'll just run your mouth and tell them all about who I am and what I'm doing. No fucking way. I'll find a place to ditch you somewhere along the highway." And, with that, he put the van in gear and slowly started to pull out of the parking lot.

"That's not fair," she screamed. When he ignored her, she continued screaming as loud as she could, bending over and twisting at the hip to kick the side of the van over and over again.

He started swearing at her, now screaming too. "You stupid cunt, knock it off. I'm trying to drive."

But she wouldn't stop screaming at an absolute maximum pitch, as she called out to the world for help, hoping that somebody, anybody, would hear her.

Then the van stopped, and out of nowhere a hard slam hit her in the face, and she cried out.

He grinned at her. "Are you trying to make my life a fucking nightmare? Is that what you're trying to do?" He shook his head. "Well, guess what, bitch? You're still in my possession, and, if you think you're fucking getting away with this, you're not. Believe me that this isn't your deal. This isn't your time to get free. No fucking way I'm letting you go now."

Suddenly the rear door opened, and somebody jumped inside with a roar. All of a sudden, her attacker was flung outside onto the pavement. He hopped to his feet, his fists coming up, and he danced right into Guilliam's fist. It took several hard blows before the asshole went down. She wiggled her way over to the edge of the door, watching as she struggled to get out of the stupid laundry bag.

As soon as Janelle got her arms free, she watched as the punk went down one more time. This time he stayed down.

Breathing hard, Guilliam turned and rushed to her and asked, "Are you okay?"

She nodded, tears rolling down her face. "I'm okay. I'm okay," she muttered, throwing her arms around him.

He held her tight and whispered, "Jeez, that was close."

"I know. It really was. I couldn't … I couldn't get him to stop. I kept screaming and crying at him to stop, but he kept driving. Then he pulled off to the side because I was screaming and kicking the walls."

"I was trailing the van, and, as I got closer, I could hear you."

"Thank God, thank God. He was going to—" She couldn't stop crying.

"I know. … I know." He held her close, even as he pulled out his phone and called somebody. She heard him, over her sobs. "I've got her. I've got Janelle. She's safe. I just need a hand out here with this asshole."

She heard voices on the phone and knew that help was on the way, and she finally calmed down enough to sag against him, her arms clutching him tightly. "What is wrong with this world?"

"There's a lot wrong with it, but, in this case, it's basically an old man who ran amok for a long time. He used his money and power to scare people into doing his bidding. Power, control, and hatred drove him to commit God-only-knows how many crimes," Guilliam explained.

She frowned. "An old man did this?"

He gave her half a smile. "Something like that. Yeah."

"What? Why?" she asked. "How the hell did he do that?"

"We're still working on it, but he had some help."

"Yeah, everybody around him probably," she muttered.

He smiled. "Definitely some people were looking after him, yes. And now some of them are claiming that they were forced."

Safe in the circle of his arms, she pondered that and nodded. "It's quite possible. But not this guy, not this one."

"What do you mean?"

She pointed to her kidnapper, the unconscious guy on the ground. "He wasn't forced to do this. He did it quite happily on his own."

Guilliam looked down at his prisoner and nodded. "You could be right."

"Oh, I'm definitely right," she murmured. "He told me that, for him, it was all about the money. He's doing this just for the money." He frowned at that, and she nodded. "I don't know what kind of money he's hoping to get, but, according to him, his granddad is supposed to leave him quite a pile of money—billions—if he took care of this one last job."

"One last job?" Guilliam repeated.

She nodded. "This one last job. According to this asshole, he's been cleaning up a lot of the things that didn't work out so well."

"He's the one who's killed everybody on base related to Mason's sniper attack?" Guilliam asked, shock in his voice.

"I don't know specifically about your four or five dead people who were involved in shooting Mason, but the jerk certainly seemed to think that he'd done enough to deserve whatever his granddad was handing out. Not only deserved it, but was owed it."

"Interesting," Guilliam muttered.

"And you can see it. This guy's a bit of an asshole anyway," she stated, glaring down at the unconscious man.

"Did he hurt you?"

"Not as you much as you might expect," she replied.

"He hit me several times but could have hurt me a lot more. When he drove off with me just now, he made it very clear that I wouldn't survive the day. So I started screaming and kicking the van. When I wouldn't shut up, that's when he stopped and started hitting me again. By then, my screams were for real too. I was just hoping that somehow somebody would hear me."

He nodded, his hand stroking her back. "I heard you," he whispered. "I was already out there looking for you, trying to figure out which van you were in or which building or which vehicle you could possibly be hidden in."

"I'm grateful that you found me. Jeez, what a nightmare." She looked up at him and added, "It's all so surreal. I'm still dealing with the fact that my mother just passed away."

"I know, and I'm so sorry, sweetheart."

"You were supposed to come right back," she stated in an accusing tone.

"I was back here—and right on time—but you had already been picked up and taken out."

"I was just sitting there in the room with my mother. That's all I was doing." She shook her head. "Just figuring out how to say goodbye, and then this asshole steps in. I glared at him, saying that I needed a few minutes with my mother. I didn't even register it was him. He just looked at me, smiled, and hit me on the head. When I woke up, I was in some laundry room in one of those big push carts. I talked to him just briefly, and, the next thing I know, I ended up out here again, in this van, where I woke up the second time."

"Good to know," Guilliam said. "The question is, do we have anybody else involved in this? I don't want anybody getting away with it, and we can't afford to have anybody coming back after Mason."

"God, I hope not," she muttered. "It's hard to believe this many people were involved as it is."

"I don't think most of them were involved by choice," he pointed out.

She winced at that and nodded. "No, I rather imagine an asshole like this one has many ways to make people's lives miserable. He's just that kind of a guy."

"And he talked to you?"

"Sure. All about how his Granddad was dying and was leaving him a ton of money, … if he did this last job. I suspect there's been an awful lot of prior jobs too. He mentioned something about *blackmail only working to a certain point*, and then people do shit that he couldn't even understand. So then he had to go clean up the mess."

"And that would probably explain Drew's death."

"My kidnapper did seem quite perturbed that the job on Mason hadn't been done, as if Mason had somebody watching over him."

"Yeah, he does, his wife," Guilliam noted absentmindedly.

"More than that though, like there may have been a reason that he hadn't been killed yet."

Guilliam nodded. "A lot of people are superstitious, and, when someone survives a close attempt on their life like Mason did, some people tend to get rattled and don't want to be involved."

"I don't get it," she said. "I don't know if I'm now classified as surviving an attempt on my life, but I won't be taking anything for granted after this."

"Not only that," he added, looking at her, speaking in a

gentle tone, "you also just watched somebody you cared deeply about pass away."

The tears started again, and she wiped them clear. "That is very true," she murmured. "It's not fair. I'm grateful that she's not suffering anymore and that I got to say goodbye, but damn." She sighed. "This is not the way I expected my day to go."

"No, and maybe it's for the best that it did end up this way," he suggested. "Just think about it. You're here. You're safe, and that asshole isn't going anywhere anytime soon, unless it's to jail."

"But you don't know if that's all the pieces, do you?"

"Right, I don't, which is why we're not taking the guards off Mason just yet."

"Does that mean I'm not safe either?"

He nodded. "We will treat it like you're not safe, just because." She looked up at him and frowned, and he shrugged. "I don't want you to go through anything like that ever again."

"Yeah, me neither," she muttered. "I'm just not sure how you could stop it, not if someone is intent on taking me out."

"I don't think that avenue will be used again, but I'm not sure," he admitted, with a sad smile at her, as he pushed the hair off her face. "When dealing with an asshole like this, unfortunately they have their own ideas about what they should or shouldn't do. Plus, he was getting desperate, or at least he was desperate." Guilliam stared off in the distance. "Until I talk to him, I won't know what the hell he is now. I need you to stay right here, while I search the van."

"No," she argued, gripping him hard. "We're not going anywhere until this guy is secured. I want your friends to come and confirm that, if anything happens, this asshole gets knocked out again. He's got a weapon in here somewhere, and I don't want to take the chance of his waking up and pulling something on both of us."

He smiled and gave her a gentle kiss on the temple. "Got it." He quickly grabbed the asshole and secured him with something he'd found in the back of the van. He looked over at her and asked, "Did he use these on you?"

She looked down to see the weird ties. "Maybe. I don't know. It was dark in the back of the van. Plus, I was in a laundry bag too. He secured me with something, both my hands and my feet. When I could hardly feel my arms, he did release the pressure so I could at least breathe and stretch them out a bit." She again looked at the ties on her kidnapper. "I guess they were like that."

Guilliam nodded, quickly securing his feet now. "He won't be going anywhere." He hopped into the van and, within seconds, had found several weapons. "Now this is interesting," he noted, showing them to Janelle. "We should get some very interesting forensic information off these."

By the time he stepped out of the van, both Jasper and Masters had arrived, with Gideon crossing the road, from where he'd just parked. With the kidnapper on the ground in front of them, Guilliam quickly explained what happened. Jasper looked over at Janelle, and she shrugged.

"I didn't do anything, honest. I was screaming for dear life," she muttered.

"It's a good thing you did," Jasper noted. "It was loud enough for this guy to hear you."

"Thank God for that," she muttered. "I don't think I could go through that again."

"And there is no need for it either." Jasper looked back

over at Masters. "How's Mason?"

"He's fine. He was awake a little bit earlier, enough for me to talk to him for a moment. He didn't stay awake for long. He's back under again now, but we'll let Tesla know that everything's okay and that we have the kidnapper."

"Maybe tell her that my mother is gone," Janelle added. "Tesla and I are friends."

"Right. I'm sorry about that."

She sniffled, then nodded. "It's all right. Considering the rest of my day, that part was normal in a way. The good news is, she's at peace now."

"And you got a chance to say goodbye, before this ass-hole snatched you," Jasper pointed out.

"Yes," she agreed, giving Jasper a haunted look. "I can't imagine how I would feel if I'd found out she had died before I was back with her."

"Thankfully that's not an issue here." Jasper turned to Guilliam. "You need to take her home."

"I will, but we have this guy to interrogate."

Jasper eyed their prisoner and stated, "We'll take him back to the office." Then he frowned at Janelle.

"I know. You want me out of the way." She raised both hands. "I'm more than happy to go home. I would like to have a hot bath, cry for a couple hours, down an entire bottle of wine, and find myself completely unconscious for at least twelve hours."

Gideon laughed. "After what you've been through, that's probably not a bad idea." He looked at the other two team members. "We need to set her up with a guard though."

"I don't get that part," Janelle pointed out. "Everything about me was an attempt to make Guilliam do something, and now that it's over with, wouldn't it be foolish for them to come back after me? Is anybody even left to do it? At what point do they just run out of bad guys?"

"I would have thought they'd run out a hell of a long time ago," Gideon replied, as he put away his phone. "But on a happier note, I now have a guard arranged. He will pick you up and take you home."

"And how do I know I can trust him?" she asked.

He smiled. "Do you know any of Tesla's friends?"

"I know a bunch of them, and most of Mason's crew."

"Would you trust them?" Gideon asked.

"Sure, that's what they do."

"Exactly."

Within minutes, another vehicle drove up, and she looked over at the driver, and then her face lit up. "Evan? Oh my gosh, I haven't seen you in forever." He grinned as he walked over. She raced into his arms, and he gave her a big hug. He looked at the others over the top of her head, and she caught the silent glances back and forth. "I know. I know, but, fine, I'll go."

"Does that mean you trust me enough to keep you safe? I'm glad if that's the case," Evan teased.

"You're not like that asshole on the ground," she muttered. She looked over at Guilliam. "I would be totally okay if you kicked the shit out of him again."

He laughed. "Not necessary, as he's not going anywhere."

"Maybe not," she agreed, "but he's definitely ruined my peace of mind, … probably for the rest of my life."

"You'll get it back," he noted calmly. "Not to worry, as this won't be the way it ends."

"You say that but …" she added.

"And I mean it too," he pointed out. "Absolutely no way

this ends like this. However, we do need to interrogate this guy. So, as much as I would love to take you home myself, I need to be here to see what the hell's going on."

"I get it," she said, with a sigh, then looked over at Evan. "Looks like you're it."

He smiled. "I am more than happy to be it. Come on. Let's get you home." And, with that, he gently put an arm around her shoulders and led her to his car.

When a shout came from behind her, she turned to see Guilliam walking toward her. She looked up at him, feeling her heart aching, whether because of him, what had happened to her with the asshole, or still about her mother passing.

He folded her in his arms, held her close, and whispered, "I'll be by later tonight, okay? We can talk then."

She lifted her tear-streaked face and shared, "I could be asleep."

"That's fine. I'm still coming by."

She gave him a smile that she knew was probably the first real smile she'd had since this nightmare began, and she nodded. "Thank you."

"This just might be a whole new beginning."

"I hope so. Whatever this ending is, it sucks." She reached out, kissed him on the cheek, and added, "I'll talk to you later." And, with that, she looped her arm through Evan's and let him walk her to his vehicle.

GUILLIAM WATCHED JANELLE leave, forcing his hands into his pants pockets instead of reaching out and snagging her back into his arms.

"I didn't think you could let her go there for a minute," Jasper noted at his side.

"I wasn't sure either," he muttered. "You know what I want to do."

"Of course. We've all been through it."

"I know." He turned back to the asshole on the ground, surprised to see him staring up at him. Such a calculating look filled his gaze that Guilliam wanted to clock him one. In fact, he walked closer and bent down.

Jasper grabbed him and muttered, "Nope. We're not doing that." When Guilliam glared at him, Jasper shook his head. "I know. Believe me that I know, but we need answers."

Their prisoner just laughed. "I'm not giving you any answers," he sneered. "Ain't nothing you can do that will get me to talk."

"Yeah? How about the fact that your dear old grandfather, the one you're counting on for all that money, is nearly broke?"

The kidnapper stared at him and shook his head. "That's not true," he cried out.

"Why do you think he's staying in that run-of-the-mill old folks' home instead of some fancy private place?"

He blinked and shook his head. "He's always been thrifty."

"Yeah, sure," Jasper quipped. "Not that the money will make a damn bit of difference to you, not from prison."

They loaded him up into one of the vehicles from the base, and then, driving his own car, Guilliam arranged to meet them back at their offices.

Hopefully they had the whole gang now, all the people involved in the sniper shooting of Mason. If he were awake right now, that would be a huge boon as well. By the time Guilliam walked into the investigative offices, he was tired, frustrated, fed-up, and incredibly short on patience. He glared at the man sitting in the prisoner box. "Seeing as you're not getting out of jail anytime soon, I want you to talk."

"That's fucking nice," the guy said, laughing at him. "Yet you ain't got me on nothing. She was in my vehicle because she wanted to be there. She was looking for a real man," he added in a mocking tone.

"Tied up, *huh*?"

"Yeah, tied up," he confirmed. "That's how she likes it. Maybe you should have tried something like that."

He studied him closely for a moment, wondering where the chink in his armor was. The guy was awfully young for that much negativity.

"If you're expecting me to talk, forget it," he said, with a wave of his hand.

"I don't expect you to talk. I know you'll talk," Guilliam replied, with a laugh. "It's just up to you how long you want to hold out."

"Ooh, what are you planning to do, beat me up?" He snorted. "You see? We're not constrained by the same set of rules that you are," he noted, with a smile. "So, there's absolutely nothing you can do to me. You can sit there and listen to nothing as long as you like, but I'm not offering anything."

"We already know everything because your grandfather is in the room next to us."

He stared, an expression of shock on his face. "Grandpa's here?"

"He sure is, and he's already told us plenty."

"Bullshit. Granddad would never turn me in."

"He already did. He gave you up immediately," Jasper interjected in a bored tone. "How do you think we found you so fast?"

He shook his head. "That's BS, absolute fucking BS. He wouldn't do that."

"Do you really think your Granddad gives a shit at this point in his life?" Guilliam asked curiously. "I mean, really? You know what your life is like. You know what his is like. So where do you see that he cares one bit about you?"

He glared at him. "That's not true. He wouldn't do that."

Guilliam shrugged. "Whatever." He looked over at the others. "Maybe we should just let the two of them have a little talk. Who knows? Maybe this asshole will kill his own grandfather for us."

He glared. "No way I'm doing that," he sneered. "And nothing you could say will make me."

"Oh, I don't know." Guilliam was laughing now. "I'm pretty-damn sure that by the time you figure out that he doesn't have you in his damn will at all—or, even if he did, there's nothing left for you to get—I think you might look at things differently."

The kidnapper just glared at him.

Guilliam asked, "Your name is Greg, isn't it?"

He nodded. "No big deal. You could have gotten that info most anywhere. Obviously you know that Granddad had two grandsons."

"We do, and both of them are pieces of shit apparently."

He stiffened at that but didn't say anything.

"And you don't like your aunt. We also know that."

"Nobody does. She's just a stuck-up bitch, and she made

my mother's life hell."

"Right. Your granddad had two daughters and no sons. Is that right?"

"Yeah. Believe me that he hated that too."

Guilliam just stared at him for a long moment. "In that case, he must have been happy to have two grandsons. Too bad your cousin Gabe turned out to be such a mess."

"Oh, he was a mess all right," Greg agreed, with a shrug. "That wasn't my doing. He was the one who was messing up all over the place."

"Yeah, so what was up with breaking into houses? That is guaranteed to get him killed eventually."

Greg shrugged. "That's what happens, isn't it? When you screw up over and over, that's what happens."

"So, Granddad didn't particularly appreciate Gabe screwing up, did he?"

"Nope, he didn't appreciate it at all. He wasn't upset at his little pastime, but he was upset that he was doing things that somebody would find out about," Greg explained. "More than that, Granddad was all about making sure the asshole who killed Gabe paid for it."

"Right. Because nobody's allowed to defend themselves when the criminal who comes calling is part of your family, right?"

"Greg glared at him. "I already told you how Gabe was a fuckup, but he was family, as my granddad would say."

"Of course, and that makes everything all right."

"No, it doesn't make it all right," Greg argued, "but I'm not changing anything at this point."

"Neither is your granddad," Guilliam said, with a laugh. "Particularly his will."

"I'm not listening to you on that," Greg snapped, with a

wave of his hand. "Granddad and I made an arrangement on that, and he's not breaking it. Of all the things he is, he's still a man of his word."

"A man of his word, *if* he had money left," Guilliam pointed out, with a smile, "but he doesn't."

"Bullshit, Grandpa's companies are worth millions."

"The companies *were* worth millions, but then your uncle made all these bad decisions. So they had to sell a whole lot to settle up the lawsuits, involving your cousin."

"Lawsuits?" he asked, frowning.

"Did you really think that all those people involved in Gabe's B&Es didn't sue him?"

"Why the hell would they do that?"

"It's called breaking-and-entering."

"But they didn't prove it was him in any of it."

"Sure, they did. They found his DNA all over the place."

Greg groaned. "Still, it wouldn't matter. I can't see Granddad paying out very much. He's not into—what would you call them, shysters? If that happened, he would have been out gunning for the whole lot of them."

"And maybe that's what you were supposed to do next."

"I wasn't about to do anything *next*. I told him that this was a done deal." Then Greg frowned. "Not that you know anything about it."

"No, of course not, but you just told us how it was a deal you made with your granddad."

He shrugged. "Doesn't matter, and Granddad's not talking."

"Oh, your granddad's talking plenty," Jasper stated, with a smirk.

With that, Guilliam walked out of the room, headed over to where Greg's granddad was held, and announced,

"We've got your grandson."

"That's nice," the old coot muttered, with a wave of his hand. "As long as he did his damn job, nothing matters."

"He seems to think that he's getting a fair amount of money from you."

The old man winced. "Yeah, I did let him believe that. He will be a little miffed when he finds out there isn't a whole lot left and what there is goes to that idiot son-in-law of mine."

"The son-in-law who runs the companies?"

"Ran them right into the ground."

"And yet he still works there, still keeps everything functioning, doesn't he?"

"Not so much. We're selling the bulk of it now, with several selling at a loss. He didn't invest in real estate, as I thought we should. He invested in a couple dot coms that burned out and hit the ground," he explained, with a groan. "So, yeah, my grandson's expecting a whole helluva lot of money, and not much money will be left at all."

At that, Guilliam smiled, returned to the grandson, segregated in his own room, and announced, "You might want to hear this." And he played his grandfather's words.

Greg stared at the cell phone, his face changing from shock to fury. "He's fucking lying," he yelled. "He's fucking lying."

"No, he's not lying now. He was lying for all these years, lying about being megarich. He might have been rich at one time, but, once you start making poor investments and selling companies because they cost more money than they were worth, plus not buying up more lucrative investments, that big stash of money ends up being a whole lot less than you thought."

"No way they would have burned through it all," Greg declared. "No way."

"Yet you're seeing this as a big chunk of money that was yours, that was due to you. Still, the money needs to be divvied up."

"But it's mine. Everything I've done was because Granddad promised that money was coming to me."

"Do you want a chance to talk to him? Of course we must be there during that conversation."

Greg glared at Guilliam. "Yeah, you're fucking right that I want to talk to him. Let me see that old geezer and let him say it to my face," he snapped. "No way that sleazeball is getting away with that shit."

And, with Jasper's help, they quickly put the two prisoners together, in the same cell but separated.

"Granddad, tell me that you were lying," Greg roared.

Granddad looked over at Guilliam and groaned. "Of course you just had to let him know."

"Let me know what?" Greg asked. "You think they haven't got it all figured out by now?"

"They don't know anything," Granddad spat. "My life is over, and I don't give a shit if I spend the next couple months in jail because I've only got a few months left anyway. But you? You're the idiot who will now be spending years in jail."

Greg stared at his grandfather and shook his head. "Tell me again that you have money out there for me," he demanded. "Don't lie to me. Tell me the truth."

"I didn't want you to find out this way," his grandfather began, "but there's no easy way to tell you. I have some money, but a lot of it goes to your aunt and uncle. They are my first responsibility."

Greg blinked at that. "What do you mean, *they* are your

first responsibility?" he cried out. "That's just bullshit."

"It's not so much bullshit," he replied, "but I do have that responsibility to them. My daughter may or may not survive much longer, but I must ensure she's got money, at least until she's dead and gone. As much as I don't like my son-in-law's business decisions, a lot of that money is already locked up in his name."

Greg slumped in place, as he stared at the old man. "And what about me?" he asked. "Where is my money in all this?"

His granddad winced. "You weren't supposed to find out until I was dead," he stated, turning his gaze to the others. "But instead these assholes had to come along and ruin everything."

Guilliam snorted. "What? You mean, ruin all your plans that included cheating your grandson out of his payday?" Guilliam asked. "How much of all this death and blackmail and corruption was just you two guys, or are other players involved too."

"It's just me," Granddad replied, but his response was a shade too quick.

Guilliam looked over at Jasper and frowned.

Jasper nodded. "You say that, but I have a gut feeling that's not quite true."

"It is true," he stated, glaring at them. "You've got no call to hassle anybody else in my world."

"We'll hassle whoever the hell we want," Jasper noted. "So don't you worry. We'll start with all those people who worked at the retirement home to see what they have to say. We'll tear apart your life and figure out just what else you're hiding."

"I'm not hiding anything," he snapped, glaring at them. "And you guys can go fuck yourself." And, with that, he fell silent and refused to say anything more.

CHAPTER 9

JANELLE SAT IN her kitchen, as she waited for a call, with an update on the scenario from Guilliam.

Evan, for the umpteenth time, patted her hand and said, "He'll be fine."

"I know he'll be fine," she muttered, with a groan. "I just want everything over with."

"I get that, but, even when it's over," he pointed out, "it won't necessarily be over. Not in the way you want it to be."

She winced at that and nodded. "Meaning that, just because they caught my kidnapper, it doesn't mean we've solved everything."

"Exactly," Evan agreed. "Are you sure your kidnapper didn't say anything that could be important?"

She pondered that and shrugged. "Honestly, I was only thinking about getting out of there alive. I wasn't listening for intel that would help with the big picture."

He chuckled. "And survival's important too. When you stay focused, you would be amazed what you can pull off."

"That's what I had hoped," she shared. "As it was, Guilliam managed to find me."

"I heard you kicked and screamed enough that people heard you from inside the van."

She chuckled. "Apparently I do have a good set of lungs on me."

He smiled at that. "And apparently Guilliam's still very important to you."

She winced. "Yes, he is." She stared off in the distance, as the reminder of why they had separated hit home again. She blinked back the tears. "I will need to make final arrangements for my mother."

"Do you know what she wanted?"

"She wanted to be cremated, and she didn't want a stone in the earth. She just wanted a little memory somewhere on a wall, someplace where I could go to and mourn. But, other than that, she just wanted her ashes spread out somewhere in nature."

"That is a lovely sentiment," he replied, "I don't even know what the law says about things like that anymore."

"I'm sure there's a law against it," she muttered. "It seems like a law stops everything you want to do these days."

His lips twitched at that. Wanting to change the subject, he got up, walked over to the fridge, and asked, "Surely there's something in here we can eat, right?"

"Are you hungry again?" she asked.

He glanced over at her. "We had a sandwich. A single sandwich."

She laughed. "Let's see what there is, and maybe we can create something. I gather we don't want to order in."

"No, I don't want to invite anyone around right now. I would prefer not to go out either, and I'm damn sure not leaving you alone."

"Right, so in that case," she said, "we need to find food for you." She checked the freezer and pondered some of the items.

He suggested, "I would be okay with just a big old omelet, and I can make it."

"Sure, if that works for you."

"It will."

She watched as he cracked six eggs and frowned at him. "Are you sharing that omelet?"

He asked, "Do you want some?"

Her jaw dropped. "Can you seriously eat a six-egg omelet by yourself?"

He raised one eyebrow and replied, "Yeah, no problem."

"Okay then. In that case, I think you need to have it all. I'm not that hungry."

He frowned and walked closer to her. "You might not be all that hungry, but you shouldn't be *not* eating either."

"No, I'm fine," she said, with a wave of her hand. "You go for it."

Then she watched as he very capably made a hefty mushroom, bell pepper, and cheese omelet, and honestly, it looked wonderful by the time he sat down with it. "I hadn't considered how much food you would need, given your size."

"Size doesn't necessarily matter, not when you're working under stress," he explained. "You need to keep your strength and energy up." He had just finished eating, when his phone rang. He checked the number and frowned as he looked at it. "No name."

"That happens though, doesn't it?"

"Sure, it happens," he agreed, still staring at his cell.

But she could tell that he didn't like it. "So we just stay here and wait until somebody we know contacts us?"

"Pretty much," he noted, with a smile. "Unless you need to go somewhere."

"I would love to go to the hospital and see Tesla and Mason."

He frowned at that. "We could do that, but only if she's up for it. If not, I don't want you anywhere around that place."

"But you think it's safe for them?"

"If it's not safe for her and Mason, then it's not safe for anybody," he stated. "Meanwhile we have extra guards there."

"Right, so that's the one place that is safe."

"It wasn't safe for you," he pointed out. "We're probably still better off staying here."

She groaned. "I hate sitting and waiting. I would much rather go to the hospital. Besides, I probably have paperwork and stuff to fill out for my mother."

"*Hmm*," he muttered. "That is possible too, isn't it?"

"I have to make arrangements for her body."

He nodded, as he looked down at his phone. "You contact Tesla and see if she's okay with a visitor, and then we can go take care of some of that stuff."

"Good," she replied, with a beaming smile. She quickly phoned Tesla, and her friend was more than happy to have her come by.

"I had a serious conversation with Mason today, more than two minutes long," Tesla exclaimed. "He's getting better. Oh my God, I could … Well, today it seemed as if he was really here and doing better."

"Excellent," Janelle said. "We'll try not to tire him if he's awake. But what about you? Do you need us to bring you anything?"

"No, I think I'm okay," she replied. "Now that I know he's out of hot water, I should be able to go home now and then and get changed."

"Good Lord, do you need us to bring you clothes?'

"No, I've got several changes with me," she explained. "It's just, there's a difference between getting changed in a small hospital room versus in your own home."

"Of course. I totally get that. Anyway, I'm not sure how long we'll be, but we should be there fairly soon."

"Good enough. If you wanted to pick up some of those muffins or a little bit of something along that line, I wouldn't object."

"Consider it done," Janelle stated cheerfully. When she got off the phone, she told him about Tesla's request.

"Right. She likes the muffins from Mario's, doesn't she?"

"I think so." Janelle frowned. "She may have other favorites as well, but Mario's has good muffins and doughnuts, and that would be a change of pace from the hospital cafeteria."

"Exactly," Evan confirmed. "We can go pick up a few things for her. She's bound to be sick of whatever food she's getting there."

"And yet she's not complaining because that is not her way."

"That's very true. I'm thrilled to hear that Mason is doing better and pulling through this."

"It's easy to say that we never expected anything else from him, yet we know how swiftly things can completely change."

Looking somber, he nodded. "That's very true. Yet he's improving, so we will stick with that and will stay positive."

"Of course," Janelle agreed. "Anyway, if you're okay to go to the hospital now, I'm ready whenever you are."

He nodded, and they got up and locked up the house.

As he led her out to the car, she could tell that he was constantly looking around.

"Even though those guys are in custody, you're still that wary?"

"I am still that wary," he declared, "because we never know for sure if other people were working with them."

"Those dead bodies you have linked to Mason's sniper are an awful lot of people already," she noted. "Surely Gabe's vengeful family are bound to run out of bad guys eventually."

He burst out laughing at that. "We keep thinking that about the evil in the world, yet they keep showing up."

She winced and didn't have anything to add. They made a detour to pick up some muffins. Janelle also grabbed some fresh coffee, some fruit, and a few other items on offer.

By the time she came back out, he asked, "Is that for us?"

She groaned. "Don't tell me that you're hungry again."

"I'm always hungry," he stated, with a fat smile.

"Never seen the likes of it," she muttered, shaking her head. "Are you sure you don't have a tapeworm?"

"That would be pretty distressing," he noted, looking at her in horror. "Why would you even suggest something like that? I'm just a growing boy."

"Yeah. It's the *growing* part that worries me," she said, with a laugh.

Back at the hospital, he parked as close to the front entrance as he could. Then, keeping an eye all around, he led her inside. He still didn't relax until they got up to the floor where Mason was, and, indeed, three guards were stationed there. Evan nodded at them and spent a few minutes speaking with them, while Janelle walked into the hospital room. She stepped inside to see Mason sleeping, but Tesla was sitting up, working on her laptop. She teased her friend. "There's got to be another way for a pregnant woman to work on a laptop."

She laughed. "You would think so, wouldn't you? Yet even with a portable laptop, they still aren't the easiest things to get a belly around."

"Of course not. Anyway, you need to relax a bit, so get off that laptop and have a fresh coffee, if that's what you want. I also brought you some tea bags and a few other things, including muffins and some fruit."

"Oh, lovely." Tesla eyed the tea bags and muttered, "I wonder how I can get water."

"Nurses station? I could go get it."

"Mason's team won't want you running around the hospital. Maybe I'll just have the coffee right now," she noted. "I haven't had any today, trying to keep my consumption down because of the baby. However, I could sure use a cup now."

As Janelle sat in the visitor's chair, she smiled at her friend. "I'm sure you've heard the update."

"I have. I also heard about your kidnapping ordeal." Tesla studied Janelle carefully. "Are you okay?"

"I'm okay, almost back to normal."

"Almost?" she asked, with a note of humor.

"An awful lot is going on in my world right now. All that time, especially these past few weeks, I've been waiting for something to happen, waiting for that inevitable time when my mother would pass on, and now that she has, I haven't even had a chance to properly grieve for her."

"I'm sorry. This all came down at a very strange time for you."

"And yet, in a way, it's the best timing. I certainly didn't expect Guilliam to be here, but get this, apparently my mother contacted him."

Tesla stared at her friend in surprise. "She did?"

Janelle nodded. "I think Mom felt it was time for him to come back into my life because Mom knew she was dying."

Tesla sat back and frowned. "She knew she was that close to death?"

"She did know apparently—or she felt it, or something. I don't know. It blows me away that she reached out to him."

"And do you know that they haven't been in contact at any other time? Any chance Guilliam was always there in the wings, just waiting?"

She stared at her. "I don't know, but that would have been very rough on him, wouldn't it?"

"Think about it. If the man loves you, and you made a hard decision that he struggled with, wouldn't it make sense that he was always right there, on the perimeter?"

"Maybe," she muttered, as she sat back and stared at Tesla. "I never considered that."

"When you get a chance, you can always ask him about it. I'm sure at this point he would tell you the truth."

"I think he would have told me the truth no matter what," Janelle replied. "That was never an issue between us. If anything, we are too blunt and too much into sharing the unvarnished truth. The thing is, I realize now that I could have given him a different answer. I could have given him a different alternative to what I did. Hell, I could have just asked him for his opinion, for his insight, with *both* of us coming to a decision. Instead I made us live very painful and lonely lives. Instead of having support at a time I really could have used it, I cut him out," she admitted, looking at her friend helplessly. "I don't get it. I just … I still don't even understand why I chose that route."

"I don't either," Tesla admitted. "Yet you did what you did, and now it's over. So you need to just accept that whatever it was, whatever reasoning you had, it was the right thing for you at the time. You'll have to let it go and move on."

She laughed at that. "I forgot how easy everything is for you."

"It's not easy at all," she declared. "Yet you do learn, over time, that answers aren't always there and that things don't always go the way you thought they would. Whenever you make plans, life can turn around and can tell you, *Nope, not happening.*"

Janelle groaned. "It's scary though, isn't it? You think everything is all set to work out one way. Then you turn around, and it's not even close. I had no idea what I would do when my mother was gone, and, ever since her death, I haven't had a moment to even blink."

"And yet, somewhere in the back of your mind, you were probably thinking you would get in touch with Guilliam at some point in time."

"Yes, definitely. But it was also very cocky of me to think that he would still be there, waiting, available."

Tesla chuckled. "Absolutely, and it is quite remarkable. Not many men would still be sitting there, waiting for you, when you made a difficult decision like that. He waited for years."

"I know, but Mom was supposed to survive," Janelle muttered. "In my head we would fight hard against the cancer, and she would beat it. Then we would all go back to normal. And instead it took far longer than I ever envisioned, and this is where we're at." She felt the tears choking the back of her throat.

Tesla reached out a hand and gripped hers. She tasted the coffee, then winced. "It doesn't taste the way I was hoping it would."

"You've probably forgotten what a good strong cup of rich coffee tastes like. No worries, just put it down. Maybe I'll drink it, or I could always give it to Evan. He's like a bottomless pit. Do you want me to get you some hot water for tea?"

She nodded. "That sounds wonderful, but I don't want to put you out."

"Nonsense, if nothing else, there's got to be a teakettle somewhere. Let me go check it out."

She stepped outside the room, and the four men who had been standing there talking, turned and glared at her. She rolled her eyes at them. "I was just going to see if a teakettle is somewhere so Tesla could have a cup of tea."

"She doesn't want the coffee?" Evan asked.

She smiled and shook her head. "No. Not now, anyway. Yet she would love a cup of tea."

"Of course."

CHAPTER 10

WITH THE TEA bag in hand, Janelle headed to the nurses' station. It was empty. She looked around to see if anybody was close by, but nobody was. Everybody appeared to be off dealing with patients. She sighed and then caught sight of a little kitchen area behind the nurses' station. Janelle hesitated, wondering how much trouble she would get into if she went in there and put on the kettle. She wouldn't want to step on any toes, but Tesla wanted a cup of tea. Surely getting a pregnant woman some hot water for tea couldn't be that big of a problem.

So she stepped around the counter and went straight back into the kitchenette area. She filled the pot with water and put it on, then stepped back out so she wasn't in the restricted area. She sat outside near the front desk and waited for a nurse to show up. When none did, she started to get worried, then heard conversation behind her, as several of them returned to the station.

One of the women asked, "May I help you?"

"I was hoping to get a cup of tea," she explained. "Nobody was here, and I apologize, but I put on the teakettle, and I hope to grab some hot water."

One of the nurses asked, "You went back there and put

it on?"

Janelle hesitated, then decided that honesty was the best answer. "Yes, I thought that somebody would be there, so I called out, stepped inside, but nobody was there. So I just put on the kettle and stepped back out of the room to wait. I've been waiting for it to boil and for somebody to come back."

The woman frowned at her and said, "This area is restricted."

"I understand that. And, if somebody had been here, I would have asked them about it beforehand."

The woman gave her an odd look, muttered something under her breath. Still, she took the tea bag and walked to the back of the kitchenette, plopped the tea bag into a cup, poured hot water on it, and brought it out to her. "That's all I can do for you. Please do not come back here again."

Her words were stiff and incredibly unwelcoming, and Janelle realized how badly she must have stepped on somebody's toes. She apologized again, took the cup, and headed back to Tesla. The rude nurse had not been out of order because Janelle had clearly been in the wrong. However, how irritating it was that she could get into trouble for something like that, when it hadn't been her intent to break any rules or to offend anyone. Obviously the rude nurse had seen it a different way. As Janelle returned, the men nodded at her, and she stepped into the room.

Tesla looked up and smiled. "You got some."

"I didn't get anything to go with it. I saw no milk, no sugar."

"Milk would be nice, but even a cup of tea is great."

As far as Janelle was concerned, a cup of tea wasn't the same if you didn't have milk. "I'll just pop down to the cafeteria and get a little pint of milk, and it should last you most of the day. Surely we can get a few more cups of tea."

"I should have just had someone get a kettle from home for my use," Tesla added, looking around. "There are certainly enough outlets available."

"We should have thought of that before, considering how long you've been here, right?"

"But you don't want to be breaking the rules because you're here, and you just want everything to go properly, all so they can focus on taking care of the patients."

Feeling sad and sorry for everything she'd gone through already, Janelle stepped back outside, looked over at the men, and announced, "I need to go to the cafeteria and get some milk for her tea."

Evan stepped up to join her. "Let's go."

As they walked past the nurses' station, the one nurse glared at her.

Once they were just out of earshot, he noted, "I gather you stepped on some toes."

"I guess." Janelle frowned. "I didn't consider it that big of a deal, but nobody was at the nurses' station or inside the kitchenette behind the nurses' station. So I put on the teakettle, and then I stepped back out and waited."

"Ah, you went into their territory."

She nodded. "Apparently that's all it took."

"Sometimes that's the case," he said, with a small smile in her direction. "As you well know, nobody likes to have their toes stepped on."

"And you're right. I just didn't think it would offend anyone so greatly." She gave him an eye roll. "Besides, if I can do something to make this easier on Tesla, I will do it," she declared.

He smiled. "It's nice that Tesla has a champion."

"As you well know, Tesla has lots of champions," she replied. "Quite a few of us have known and have loved her for many years," she murmured. "We are all so busy in our lives, it's hard to always stay in touch the way we would want to, but, when something like this happens, we all come out of the woodwork."

He smiled. "And that's how it should be. Friends helping friends."

"And that's why you're here, isn't it?" she asked, with a sideways look at him.

"Yeah, it is. I've known Mason for a very long time. I've served with him for years, and we've been through some challenging times together. It breaks my heart to see him like this."

"And yet we both know this is temporary, especially for somebody like Mason."

He chuckled. "The only problem with that thinking is, when anyone does die, it just shocks the hell out of us."

"And yet we all die at some point," she muttered, a pang of fresh pain going through her.

He murmured, "I'm sorry. I forgot about your mom."

"No, that's what we're supposed to do, right? We're supposed to move on. We're not supposed to have a heart attack, or to melt down every time somebody mentions death or dying, or what we do afterward," she shared, giving herself a shake. "Everybody's been very kind to me. It's just been such a shock, what with all this extra stuff going on. So I don't even know how to react anymore. You just see everything happening around you, and you react blindly, without thinking about what you're saying and what you're doing. It's just this instinctive movement that you make."

She sighed. "So, I'm sure I could be doing lots of other things right now, but I guess I'm still feeling very much like I'm in shock."

"So, you should be," Evan stated. "Not only did you just lose your mother after many years of illness but you've just successfully survived a kidnapping that could have ended very badly. So, don't judge yourself so harshly."

She gave him a sideways glance, her lips twitching. "It's almost as if you know women."

He rolled his eyes. "I'm married to a pilot," he reminded her, with a smile. "And I understand a whole lot of things, not only about women, but about people now, too," he shared. "She has given me incredible insight into a world that I hadn't really recognized as being an issue. However, when you deal with people under trauma or a stress of some kind, as you have been," he pointed out, "all kinds of shit happens, and you don't really have a chance to react to anything. You literally just go through the motions. Your body is functioning, and your mind—although it's numb in many ways—somehow just keeps functioning too."

They walked into the cafeteria, and he asked, "Do you want anything?"

She looked at everything and sighed. "Maybe a cup of tea."

He laughed. "In that case, why didn't we just come and get Tesla's cup of tea from here?"

"I don't know." Janelle groaned. "Getting it up on her floor just seemed like a good idea at the time."

"And because you were just helping her."

"Still, that nurse will not remember me kindly."

"I don't remember seeing that nurse before," he noted, "although I haven't been here enough to keep track of the nurses."

"That's the thing, right? They have so many people on staff, yet still must have shortages and must rely on traveling nurses and sharing between departments, so you never know who's who," she noted. "You just hope that everyone who comes through is supposed to be here."

"Which is also why the hospital must have as many security checks as they do."

She rolled her eyes at that. "And do you think they do?" she asked. "Or is that just another fallacy?"

"God, I hope not, because there must be some security in place here."

"Sure, there are key cards, but what if their key cards are stolen or don't work or something?" she asked, looking at him. "I can't imagine they have a whole lot else in place."

"No, those cards could be everything, couldn't they?" Evan asked, as he calmly looked out at the world around them.

They moved to the counter in the cafeteria and quickly bought several cups of tea. He grabbed a coffee for himself, and they headed back up to Tesla again.

"You seem preoccupied," she murmured, as they made it to the floor where Tesla was waiting.

"It's not so much that I'm preoccupied, but we've come up against things like this in the past. We just never have a good idea of who's involved in these kinds of actions," he admitted. "So, we're at a loss sometimes as to how to stop it, outside of posting guards."

"Yes, but you and I both know, when personnel have to go in and out of hospital rooms to tend to the patients, if somebody's up to no good and wants to get in, they'll get in."

He glared at her. "Now, why would you be putting that shit in my head?"

She smiled at him. "Oh, come on. I didn't put that in your head. It was already there, and you know it. You were just assessing the danger of leaving Mason and Tesla alone with just three guards."

"And yet three guards should be plenty."

"Yes, they should be." Then she stopped as she reached the area where the trio of guards stood, talking. "You trust these men, right?"

He nodded. "Yes, Jasper has been careful to see that they're all men we've served with, and Mason has served with."

"And none of them have a grudge against him that you know of?"

"No," he stated, staring at her.

She shrugged. "Then, if we don't see an inside attack like that, it must be somebody who can get close enough to Tesla. And if that's not somebody she knows and trusts, it's got to be somebody she doesn't know or somebody who she doesn't expect to see."

He looked at the door. "Like a nurse?"

GUILLIAM THREW HIMSELF into a nearby chair and glared at Jasper. "Supposition is fine and dandy, but we need proof, proof that somebody else is involved, proof of what their actions are likely to be, now that we have the grandfather and Greg in custody. Will the others just walk away, hoping to stay uninvolved, or is that need for revenge so strong that they will go after Mason anyway?"

"We can't afford to be wrong on somebody else's being involved."

"No, we can't. Plus, we're running out of suspects." They pondered that for a bit, before Guilliam spoke up again. "Both grandsons are accounted for, one dead and one in lockup here. There is Gabe's mother, who's going through cancer treatments, and we've got Gabe's father, who is running the businesses. He's been a big force in town, but he doesn't seem to share the same attitudes as his deceased son, his nephew, or his father-in-law."

"I'm not sure if anybody has that kind of force in the community, outside of this old coot," Jasper noted. "When you think about it, how many assholes in the world can continue like this, without seeing the writing on the wall? It's one thing for the old codger to behave in that way—he's been getting by with it for at least seventy years—but with the son-in-law taking over the reins, the business changing, his living at the retirement home, no wonder the grandfather was desperate now to finish off Mason."

"Right, and the son-in-law made several decisions that weren't good for the business."

"Or maybe it was good for the business, but, because of the grandfather's methodology, everything changed, and maybe his methods were no longer working."

"Exactly. So who does that leave?"

"Just the daughter with cancer and her husband, at least alive and out of jail."

"Or anybody that the grandfather may have paid as a backup. Contracts don't necessarily get shut down just because a person has died or has been picked up and thrown in jail. It would remain a contract until the deed was done."

Jasper nodded. "That's true, but how will we figure it

out? I don't think either of these family members are too interested in telling us."

"Don't you think the grandson might have something to say, now that he knows he's not getting the big windfall he'd expected?"

"I don't know if deep down he ever believed he would get the big money, or if he understood how much they didn't have," Jasper murmured. He looked back at the temporary jail area. They were waiting for an escort to take the two men to local police jail cells, so the prisoners were safely ensconced somewhere else, and the navy investigative team didn't have to be on guard all the time.

Guilliam continued. "It's a very strange scenario. I get the grandfather, and I get the grandson. If that's the end of the attacks on Mason from that family, this would be lovely, but I'm sure not getting that same feeling from either of them."

"No, I'm not sure either. Again, the old man is implying that it's not over, but then he's not saying anything specific either. It's almost as if he doesn't want us to know something. Yet he's reassuring himself that he's still got an ace in the hole—and one that we've got to watch out for."

"Agreed, but I'm not sure how we're supposed to track this unknown entity. Yet we better do it before it becomes something else."

"You mean another attack?" Jasper asked.

"Exactly," Guilliam stated. "We need to tear apart both of their lives—just in case," he murmured. "We can't discount the possibility of somebody else being involved, somebody the old coot has been using on the sly, like a hitman, for want of a better word. The invisible muscle. That one person he potentially kept as a hidden weapon."

"And that's great, but who would have seen him?"

"We should check every person who's visited him at the retirement home. That would be a start. Can we pull his phone records for … what, the last year?"

Jasper's eyebrows shot up as he contemplated that idea. "It would be a hell of a lot of data, but you're right. That should be long enough for us to find out something. Let me see what I can do. You should go see Janelle."

"I would, except they're at the hospital. She wanted to go visit with Tesla."

He winced at that. "Why?" he asked in alarm.

"I thought it was a reasonable idea, just from the standpoint of getting her past what she'd been through at the hospital. So she didn't just see it as the place where she was attacked."

"You're right," Jasper conceded, "but, from a mission point of view, they're all now in one place."

"Yeah, I did think of that, but we still have three guards on Mason, so I thought maybe they would be safe. That and the fact that there is no need for anybody to come after Janelle anymore."

"I agree with you there, but I'm not sure we're dealing with logic in this instance, or even sanity. We've got revenge that's been sitting and festering for too long. A man has lost his own power, his own ability to do all the things that he's been doing all these years in order to run the world as he wanted to, and he's run amok within this community for decades. People think he has money, and he's found ways to frighten people into doing his bidding, but we have no idea just how far he's gone or what he's done with it all."

"Right. I was just wondering if we had a way to get him to talk. We can't afford to have him give up anything in terms of punishment."

"And yet think about it. What punishment will we dish out to him? What is he, eighty? He could spend the last years of his life behind bars, sure, but I don't think he's all that healthy."

"No. From the looks of him, chances are, he won't make it to trial. And that just makes it even more important to ensure we get all the information from him that we can. There won't be any going back if we wait too long, and then he dies."

"You go try talking to him again," Jasper suggested, "and I'll get the subpoenas going. Then we'll talk to the manager of the retirement home. Masters is in there talking with him now. Plus, he's got the assistant manager and a few others he's been interrogating."

Just then Masters joined them. "The manager is crumbling fairly quickly, though I'm not sure it'll do him much good. He's been facilitating the purchase of burner phones and phone cards for a couple years now. He thought the old man was just having fun playing at some spy game."

"And how is he feeling about that now?"

"He's terrified that he's on the hook for some of this."

"And he very well may be. It was against the rules of the home, so he knew it was wrong from that standpoint at least."

"Sure, but he ran the home, so, from his perspective, I doubt that he thought anything of it. Now, the other manager, she's terrified as well, and she's been coughing up all kinds of information. I'm just not sure any of it's helpful. It's a classic case of give absolutely every little detail to appear cooperative," he shared, with a wry look, "so she doesn't give up anything useful."

"Let me go talk to her," Guilliam stated, as he stood up.

Masters nodded. "Gideon is in the process of talking to the other residents of the retirement home now. So, there's a good chance he might pop up with something. Even just a little tidbit could help. What we're looking for is another person, someone who may have been involved, even as a backup. We just can't afford to miss anybody."

"I'm right there with you," Guilliam replied. "So far, the only people who visited Granddad were his daughter and his son-in-law. Though they visited just a couple times, it didn't go very well, with lots of yelling and blame. Then the grandsons visited more. It was both grandsons for a while, but, with the death of Gabe, it's down to just Greg now."

"Interesting," Masters murmured.

"In what way?" Guilliam asked.

"I guess, if you don't have a whole lot of friends all your life, nobody comes see you at that age."

"I think it's more a case of outliving most of them," Masters noted. "The other thing is, granddad seems to have been the kind of guy who made sure that he had no friends. Nobody could betray him then, right?"

"I guess," Guilliam murmured. He looked down the hall where the old man was temporarily held. "So, who is he protecting?" He turned to the others. "Any bastard children?"

"Not that we found so far," Jasper shared, "but, considering how he treated everybody in his world, including his own family members, I wouldn't be shocked at the possibility."

"Then is it anybody we know of, or is there literally somebody that he's managed to keep secret all these years?"

At the end of the day, they had talked to dozens more

people, written up statements, compared statements, and still they couldn't come up with any other person of interest. The grandson, Greg, after Guilliam and others had spoken to him several more times, had just shrugged.

"I don't know what the hell you're looking for," Greg muttered. "It was me all the time. I'm still pissed off at Granddad about that."

"If he lied about the money, would he have lied about other stuff?"

Greg stopped and glared at Guilliam, then his shoulders slumped. "I wouldn't have thought so, but now? … Now I'm not so sure."

That was honest at least, and Guilliam could understand why the young man was upset. When you spend your life acting on very risky decisions to help out, expecting to get a massive payday sooner or later, only to find out that massive payout will never happen, that was bad enough. But to also find out how dear old granddad was counting on dying before any of it came to light as far as Greg was concerned, that had to be a terrible shock.

"He was such an asshole," Guilliam said, watching Greg. "He was supposed to be dead by the time you found out that no money was left for you. Guess we ruined that for him. … So is your granddad's impending death the reason that he wanted revenge now, some four years after Gabe was killed?" It made sense to Guilliam, but he wouldn't mind getting it confirmed.

The younger man just nodded, but he didn't say anything.

"If you've got anything to say, this would be a good time to clear the air."

He waved his hands. "I got nothing to say."

"Even though your granddad will die in jail?"

"Granddad will go to jail," he stated, with a snort. "You think I won't?"

"Of course you will. After all, you did murder several people."

He winced and stared off into the distance. "It's not murder when you're just fixing problems," he muttered, "and they were all problems that needed to be fixed."

"Do you think the families of those dead people saw it that way?"

He shrugged. "I don't give a fuck about those families. My family is completely screwed up." He seemed fed up and pissed off.

"Sounds like it. What about your aunt? Is she the same?"

"She's already messed up and a royal bitch besides. I told you that." He turned and glared at him. "Go ahead and blame her for all this, as if that will be of any value. She's very sick with cancer and can't do anything anyway," he snapped. "And, when it comes to business, she never could do anything."

"How did the death of her son affect her?"

"How do you think?" he asked, looking at him in disgust. "She went off the rails. Her only kid, her perfect little boy. Christ, that guy was a complete fuckup. If he just hadn't gotten involved with Mason, he probably would have been fine."

"And yet do you think he would have just gotten worse, gotten more adventuresome in his little escapades?"

"Maybe. Granddad was trying to straighten him out."

"So, your grandfather knew?"

"Sure, he knew, but he hadn't told my cousin that he knew all about it. So, the idiot just continued to do his little stunts, thinking Granddad didn't know. He thought that Granddad might know small parts of it, but nothing that mattered." Greg shook his head. "That's the thing. Granddad always had a backup plan, and he always knew shit about everybody. I don't—I don't even know how he did it.

"Take me for instance. I cheated on a test one time way back in high school. He told me that it wasn't the time to cheat, that the time to cheat was when it really mattered, and that doing shit like that was a waste of energy. And I could get caught and damage my reputation, when it shouldn't even be impacted by something so dumb. He basically told me to get in, to do the work, and to get out. And when you cheat, make sure it's something that you really need to cheat on because there's no other option. You get in, get the job done, and you get out," he repeated, with a shake of his head. "That was Granddad's model all the way through. Get the job done and get out, and nobody else needs to know."

"Which, when you think about it," Guilliam replied, "sounds like exactly what he taught you."

"Sure. But what he's teaching me now is that, in the end, family just screws you over too."

"Which isn't a bad lesson to learn in this case because that is what happened. So now you have choices. You can hold it against him, you can get over it, or you can tell us some more. It doesn't matter because obviously you're not going anywhere but jail for a very long time."

"See? That's what's fucked up because it's just not fair. I lived up to my end of the bargain. I never even cheated again in school," Greg wailed. "It was all about being fair and honorable at that point in time, honoring Granddad's wishes. But, in the end, he didn't give a shit."

"No, it sounds like he was all about manipulating his

world to make it happen just the way he wanted it to."

"Yeah, you're not kidding." Greg stared at him. "How did this get so fucked up?"

"Either he decided that you weren't doing a good-enough job or that somebody else could do a better job."

Greg stiffened at that. "What? That's just bullshit. I was doing a damn-good job."

"So why would he have had somebody as a backup, for *just in case* then? What if you got killed? Would he have left it to chance? No way. He had a backup plan."

With that, Greg frowned. "You're right. No way he wouldn't have. Killing Mason was all that mattered to him. It's what he intended to happen, whether Granddad lived or not."

"Okay," Guilliam replied cautiously. "Then if you got killed, who would have been his backup?"

Greg just stared at Guilliam and eventually shook his head. "I have no idea. It never even occurred to me that it would be the case with me. However, what you just said makes a lot of sense."

"Why don't you help yourself and us by thinking about who he would have used as your replacement."

"Nobody," Greg declared. "You don't understand. I've been doing this for him for years. He didn't need anybody else, and he knew it."

"Right, but things were getting dicey. More dead bodies showed up, connected to Mason's sniper attack, and so your granddad would have known that it was getting harder and harder to keep a lid on things. Plus, you kept failing."

"I didn't fail," Greg snapped, glaring at Guilliam.

Guilliam changed his approach. "No, not you personally, but those people you were taking out had failed. And your granddad would have seen it that way, right?"

He shrugged. "I don't know, but Granddad wasn't happy. Things were going on that worried him. They weren't going down the way he wanted them to."

"That's what I mean. So, taking that into consideration, who else could he have called on? Somebody at the home?" he asked questioningly. "Somebody in the family?"

"There is no other family," Greg muttered, with a wave of his hand.

"What about—does your grandfather have any illegitimate kids?"

The grandson stared at him in shock. "No. At least I don't think so."

"But you don't know so, do you?"

He slowly shook his head. "No, I guess not. And in a sick way that could have been something he would do, but it would also take somebody he had to train almost as long as me," Greg explained. "And I don't know anybody along that line."

"But that doesn't mean it's not possible."

"Sure. But that's like saying his sickly daughter could have done it. It's not impossible, but it's not very plausible."

"Right." And that did make a difference.

CHAPTER 11

A S JANELLE NEARED her house, she turned to Evan, who was driving. "I haven't heard from Guilliam."

"I'm pretty sure he's on his way here now, bringing food too."

She beamed. "Now that's lovely."

"Why?" he asked curiously. "It's not as if you're eating much."

She shrugged. "No, but I am getting hungry."

"That's good to hear. You don't eat more than a mouse."

"Hey, I eat a lot more than a mouse, at least two mice."

He rolled his eyes at her poor joke, as he parked in her driveway, then motioned toward her house.

"Don't you wanna check it first?" she teased. "Maybe a boogeyman is inside."

"Good idea. Sit in the car. Keep it locked and wait until I give you the all-clear signal."

"Oh, brother," she muttered. "I guess I had that coming."

"Yep, you sure did."

He quickly left the vehicle, and she sat inside, waiting. She wasn't even sure why she'd brought it up, except for the fact that she still had that underlying fear that this wasn't over. The way everybody was acting, they didn't think it was over either, and she didn't want to be the punchline. When he came back out a few minutes later, he gave the all-clear signal.

She walked up to him. "I guess that was foolish of me. Sorry."

"No, not at all. That complacency is what we must watch out for. It becomes way too easy for people to forget and to relax their guard. So, if somebody else is involved—which we don't have any proof of at this point—we still need to keep our guard up."

"That's the thing, isn't it? How do you ever know when it's over?"

"We don't. We've got the grandfather being very cagey at the moment, and that's part of the problem. Yet nobody knows of anybody else being involved. We're doing a full search of his phone records and his visitor logs, but, so far, there doesn't appear to be anybody else."

"Then it comes down to possibly a love child thing," she murmured.

He nodded. "So, I gather you've talked to Guilliam."

"Guilliam, no, I told you that I hadn't. Yet it makes sense. The old man had zero respect for women, so staying faithful to his wife was hardly something that he cared about. He would have done whatever he saw fit. And since she only gave him two kids, and girls at that, he may very well have wanted more. Plus, since he doesn't value women, he would have wanted sons."

"That's possible," Evan agreed, "but, if that is the case, why haven't we seen them yet?"

"I don't know. Maybe he doesn't have a relationship with anyone else, or maybe the mothers were a stronger influence, and he couldn't push them around in the same way. And, if any other children did exist, he probably didn't want anyone to know about it. He was a very secretive man, and, if he could keep people guessing, he would."

Evan nodded. When his phone rang a little bit later with a text, he shared, "That's Guilliam. He's on his way."

"Good." She smiled at Evan. "Does that mean you get to go home?"

"I'm not sure what Guilliam's planning yet, so we'll wait and see."

She took that to mean no. She nodded. "In that case I'll make up the spare bed." When he began to argue, she shook her head. "You need to sleep sometime, Evan."

"I do," he conceded, with a nod. "Thank you."

She went upstairs to the spare room, quickly put on fresh bedding, and added towels to the bathroom.

As she headed back downstairs again, he asked, "Is this your house?"

"It was Mom's first house here. I lived nearby in an apartment and worked at the hospital, while I was dating Guilliam. Mom found another house to buy and gave me this one. However, when her illness got so advanced, she sold her second house to help pay her medical bills and moved out of state into a small apartment, all to be closer to her specialist and the cancer treatment facility. At that point, I quit my job to be her caretaker. She was living three states away, so I thought about selling this house too. Yet Mom talked me into renting it out to make up for my loss of income, also giving me a home to return to, hopefully with her moving back here too. She even found a property manager for me, so it wasn't something I had to deal with so much."

"No other siblings?"

"No," she murmured. "No other siblings."

"I'm sorry," Evan said. "It's a hard time to be alone."

She sniffed back the tears that once again threatened and nodded. "If I could just stop being such a watering pot, it would be a lot easier."

"Give yourself a break," he suggested. "It's only just happened, and then you were kidnapped and your life threatened only moments later. You will find that the tears come and go for quite a while yet."

"Great," she muttered. "I was hoping you would tell me how I could get over it fast."

"Nope. And the more you love them, the harder it is," he added.

She nodded and quickly busied herself, tidying up the kitchen. When Evan opened her front door, she watched Guilliam walk in, carrying several bags of food. She joked, "Oh, obviously you know Evan pretty well."

Guilliam laughed. "Absolutely I know Evan." He put the bags on the counter, walked over to her, and wrapped her into a hug. She sighed as she melted against him and cuddled up close. "Sorry I couldn't be with you today," he murmured. "Today of all days is when you needed somebody."

"Honestly, it doesn't feel real," she noted. "None of it does."

"Of course not, but it will over time, and all of this will fall into place."

"So, you say," she quipped, with a laugh. "I'm not sure I believe it."

He nodded. "I'm staying here for the night, unless you've got a problem with that."

"No, I don't. What about Evan?"

"He's been looking after you all day, so he needs a break. I could send him home, unless you have a problem with that."

"No, of course not. I didn't know what his schedule was, so I just made up the spare bedroom for him."

"Ah." Guilliam turned to Evan, who had walked into the kitchen. "Do you want to stay for the night or take off and do your own thing?"

"I'm staying for the night," he replied easily. "I figured I would take her up on the offer of a spare room. Then you can stand watch, while I get some sleep. Afterward we can switch."

"That sounds lovely to me," Janelle shared. "Thank you for staying."

Evan shrugged easily. "That's what friends are for."

"Maybe so," she muttered. "I guess I've just never had those kinds of friends before."

"It's a different world now," Evan stated, giving her a smirk. "Besides, you don't eat much. So, as long as I'm around you, I get plenty of food."

She rolled her eyes at that and told Guilliam, "The amount of food this man eats is shocking."

"Hey, I'm a growing boy," Evan stated, patting his flat stomach.

"Right," she muttered. She looked over at Guilliam. "I sure hope you brought lots of food."

"I did. I know what this guy is like. He's a legend." Guilliam motioned at the food. "I suggest we eat while it's hot." Then he looked at his watch and winced. "I'm a whole lot later than I expected. Sorry about that."

"But did you come up with anything?" she asked.

As they served up the food, Guilliam launched into an

explanation of everything they had found so far.

When he was done, she frowned. "So … that's the long way of saying no?"

He gave her a lopsided grin, as Evan chortled, nearly choking on a huge mouthful of food.

"Let's just say," Guilliam replied, "that we don't have any proof anybody else is involved, but none of us are terribly satisfied that there isn't somebody else."

She winced. "Okay, so that's not good news then."

"But it's not bad news," he pointed out. "It just gives us a little more time to figure out if anybody else is involved."

"Then it also depends on whether the person is a male or female," she added.

"But it doesn't really," Evan clarified. "Women do kill and kill a lot. Not as often, not as ugly, but they're still killers," he shared. "So if the grandfather has a granddaughter out there gunning for us, it won't be somebody you're expecting."

"That sucks," Janelle muttered. "We won't see it coming."

"You'll never see it coming," Evan repeated. "That's the whole point of this type of assassination. They happen when you've relaxed your guard."

She stared at him slowly and nodded. "And that's why you're spending the night, isn't it?"

His lips twitched into a lopsided grin. "Let's just say, I don't want anything to happen to you."

Tears collected in her eyes, and she whispered, "Thank you."

Guilliam handed her a plate of food. "Come on. You need to get some sleep tonight, so eat up now."

"Wouldn't sleep be nice. Every time I close my eyes,

guess what I see?"

"You see an asshole, who decided to play with your life," Guilliam replied. "I get it, and I'm sorry."

"It's hardly your fault, so you can't keep apologizing for something like that."

"It is my fault," he declared. "If I hadn't been in your life, your kidnapper would never have made you a target."

"Maybe. But what will you do? Sit there and apologize for the rest of your life?"

"Maybe," he said cheerfully. "At least until this is over."

She groaned, then nodded. "Fine, but I still don't think you're responsible."

They sat down to eat what appeared to be Greek dishes, but she was wolfing it down so fast that she hardly even noticed the flavor.

He patted her hand and said, "It will be all right."

She groaned, then sat back. "I'm a mess, aren't I?"

"No, you're not. You're doing fine. You've just been through a lot, so give yourself a break."

She nodded and didn't say anything. She looked over at the two men, as they finished off their first servings and went back for seconds. "I don't know where you put it all," she muttered, as she sat back, sighing. "I'm done."

Evan gave her a fat smile. "That's what we're counting on." With that, he quickly divvied up the rest of the food, and the two men both had heaped-up plates again.

She just watched in astonishment as the food disappeared. "Good for you," she muttered. "At least now I know that, if I ever invite you over for a barbecue, I need to get a whole cow."

Evan agreed with a nod. "You probably do. On the other hand, I might bring wine."

"That would be nice. How come we don't have wine now?" she asked, looking around her kitchen. "I don't even know if I have any."

"We won't be drinking while we're on duty anyway," Guilliam noted.

She rolled her eyes at that. "Thanks for the reminder."

"You're welcome." He chuckled. "And don't worry about it, we're all good."

"I'm glad you're all good," she muttered, "but now you've got me worried again."

"And you can just stop worrying too," he pointed out.

"Is it that easy?"

"You've got two highly skilled and experienced men looking after you tonight," Guilliam declared. "So I'm saying, yeah, it is that easy. At least for tonight."

She smiled, got up, and quickly cleaned the dishes, while the two men finished off their meals and then checked outside. Finding nothing to indicate the presence of visitors or anybody watching, they sat down to share more details of their day. By the time they were done eating and talking, it was almost 10:00 p.m.

She looked at them and announced, "I'm heading up to bed."

"Good idea," Guilliam said. "I'll come up in a bit."

She nodded, walked upstairs, and headed for the shower. She wasn't even sure what he meant by that. However, with Evan in the spare bedroom, the only other bedroom in her house was hers. Of course that's where he would stay. She didn't want him to stay anywhere else. Yet they weren't quite there yet. They hadn't had a chance to address any of the remaining issues between them.

However, it didn't feel as if anything was left to resolve.

It was like taking a step back in time, where somebody had stopped the clock for the last three years, while she took care of something important to her. Now the clock moved forward rapidly, leaving her stunned at the shift in her world, because it was like her old world was literally back again.

When she stepped out of the shower, she quickly dried off, got ready for bed, and curled up under the covers. About twenty minutes later, Guilliam showed up.

"Still awake?" he asked.

"I am," she murmured. "I wasn't sure if you needed to talk when you came up."

"No, I'm fine, but I will have a shower, if you're okay with that."

"Go for it," she murmured.

He'd spent many a night in this house with her. Still, it seemed strange to have him back. Yet, once again, it seemed normal.

When he came back out with just a towel wrapped around his waist, he noted, "I didn't bring an overnight bag."

She got up, headed to the bathroom, and brought out a spare toothbrush for him. "You can use this at least." She set it out on the bathroom counter, still in its packaging. He nodded, as she returned to bed and got comfortable again.

He walked over, sat down on the side of the bed with her, and said, "Hi."

She let out a burble of laughter. "Hi." She smiled up at him. "It feels very strange and yet very familiar to have you here."

He nodded.

"Before you say anything," she began, "I want to ask you a question."

He stiffened slightly and then nodded. "Go ahead."

"My mother."

He asked curiously, "What about her?"

"Did she keep in contact with you over these three years, outside of just recently?"

He nodded. He picked up her hand and explained, "She reached out to me right from the beginning. She apologized for taking you away from me."

She stared at him, wordless, her thoughts overwhelmed, wondering what made her mother do something like that.

Guilliam continued. "Your mother understood why you were doing it, and she admitted to me how she felt selfish enough to want you there for the journey because she didn't think she was strong enough to do it on her own," he shared. "She asked me to let you go long enough to help her through the initial stages. She told me how she was pretty sure she would be okay down the road, and then I could have you back."

Janelle slumped into the bed and stared at him, her tears welling up and spilling down her cheeks.

He smiled. "It's okay. She did it with the best of intentions, and out of fear of what was happening to her in her world. I understood that part. I didn't understand why you felt like a relationship with her had to be exclusive of a relationship with me, and that was the part that I suffered with. However, you made a decision and were pretty adamant about seeing it through."

She nodded. "I did. I was. But, as she told you, it was never intended to be long-term."

"Of course not," he said, "but we never know about these things in life, do we?"

"No," she whispered. "God, I feel so bad."

"Why?" he asked curiously.

"Because basically she was asking you to hang on, to wait, and that, as soon as she was done, she would give me back to you. Instead it dragged on and on and on. Yet you still waited, still put your own life on hold."

He shrugged. "I tried to move on, but you were always there in the back of my mind. I dove myself into my work and took an overseas assignment to get farther away. I got angry and tried to use the anger to force myself out into another world," he explained. "It worked for a while, but then, well, it just didn't work anymore."

He smiled and added, "Sometimes you just realize that there is only one person for you, and, if you're lucky, it works out. And, if you're not lucky, well, it doesn't," he stated. "I'm hoping that now, maybe your commitment will be to yourself and to us, not just your mother."

She put her arms around his neck and hugged him close. "Yes," she whispered. "God, yes." She leaned back ever-so-slightly and added, "There were a lot of times when I cried because of the decision I made, knowing that I had to let you go. It just wasn't fair to keep you on a string like that, but I desperately wished that you would be waiting for me, but I knew I didn't have any right to ask."

"And yet your mother did," he stated, with a wry look in her direction.

"She never told me. She never once said a word about it."

"She apologized somewhere along the line, when her treatments weren't going so well, asking if I was okay to hold on a little bit longer. She thought she could beat it. One of the last messages I had from her was that she couldn't beat it after all, that she was done fighting, and that it was time for her to accept the inevitable. Still, she hoped that I would be there because this was not the answer she had hoped for. That was a much harder journey for you, so she wanted me to be there for you."

He swallowed, then faced her fully. "I had a couple short-term relationships. However, that last message from your mother was the clincher, making me realize that, no matter how many times I tried and failed at other relationships, I wouldn't ever walk away from you." He shrugged. "That is also why I was so angry when I first saw you because nobody wants to spend years waiting for somebody who had intentionally excluded you from their life. Your mother was an awesome person. I had no problems with her, and I wouldn't have had any problems with your being there for her," he said. "It was the part about excluding me back then—"

"I know," she admitted, interrupting him by placing her finger on his lips. "It was all about why did I have to cut you out of my life to help her? I'm not sure I have an answer for you. Maybe I figured the long-distance relationship wouldn't work for us," she replied softly. "Yet I made a decision for both of us, without giving you a chance to share your own opinion. I see that now, but I never saw it before. That's the God's honest truth," she muttered.

"It's hardly something that I can explain. It was just this overwhelming emotional need to give back to my mother, after all those years of her giving her life to raise me as a single mom," she said. "She fought me over this decision time and time again, but I just wouldn't listen. I was hell-bent on doing the *right thing*, and now that her life is over, somehow it feels like all those years have just disappeared, in a way."

"And yet they haven't," Guilliam argued. "They're still there in some ways, and there is still this wall between us that needs a bit of clearing."

"The only thing I can think of to clear it," she said, "is to apologize, yet again."

"That is the last thing I want. I understood what you did. I didn't necessarily like it, and I sure as hell didn't like the part that involved my being left behind, but I am proud of the fact that you helped your mom through this period in her life, regardless of how it ended up. At the end of day, she was a wonderful woman, and I'm sorry that she had such a hard time."

Janelle sniffled again, and he smiled.

"I'm really not trying to make you cry."

"Doesn't take much to make me cry, particularly today."

He just held her close. "I know it's not good timing, and the final arrangements for your mother still need to be made and all that, but I would very much like a chance for us to start a relationship again."

Hearing those words that she had desperately wanted to hear for so long, she burst into tears and just held him close. When she could finally talk, she whispered, "Yes, please." Looking up at him with her tear-streaked face, she nodded. "God, yes. It's all I've ever wanted."

He leaned down and kissed her gently. But that small and gentle act ignited a firestorm that blew them both away. When he finally lifted his head, he was gasping hard for air. "Jeez," he muttered.

"I know. I'm sorry. It's been a long time for me."

He held her close. "It's not even about time. It's all about us and what we always had, that joy, that wonderful sense of togetherness," he murmured. "That knowing how we were exactly where we were meant to be."

And she knew that once again he was thinking of all the years he had spent without her because of her own stubbornness. "I'm so sorry."

He leaned over and kissed her hard. "That's enough of that. We don't need to keep apologizing for something that has now changed and has turned into something very different. Now it's our time."

And this time when he kissed her, she found herself flat on her back, her nightgown tossed to the floor, and her thighs spread wide, ready for him, almost as if by magic. She groaned as his fingers slipped into the moist curls below. She twisted beneath him, gasping, crying out in both joy and urgency.

He murmured, "Take it easy. We have all night."

"No," she whispered. "You have all night. Me? I've been wanting this way too long."

And when he lowered his head and suckled on one nipple, her world exploded, tightening around his body, her thighs clenching him tight as she came apart in his arms.

As she relaxed afterward, he muttered, "That's a good start." Then he rose up over her, sliding gently inside, making her shudder and come apart all over again.

"Dear God," she whispered. "That's always been where you belonged."

Those words seemed to send him into an explosion of movement as he pounded deep into the heart of her, coming apart with his own orgasm right afterward. With his release, she came apart for a third time. He groaned as he settled beside her, pulling her up close. "I'd forgotten how responsive you were."

"It's probably way more right now," she murmured,

"just because it's something I so desperately want."

"We have all night, but you do need to get some sleep."

"And so do you." She chuckled, as she curled up in his arms. "But this moment, I don't ever want it to end."

"And it doesn't have to. You don't have any more parents to look after, right?" he teased.

She chuckled. "No, no. Like you, I'm an orphan now." And once again the tears threatened to choke her.

He tapped her gently on her chin. "But you're not alone because now we'll build a life for just the two of us. We'll create our own family and have everything that we ever wanted together," he murmured. "It's all good. It's all about our tomorrows."

And with that thought, she fell asleep in his arms.

GUILLIAM WOKE WITH a start to a harsh whisper.

"Move," Evan said.

Guilliam bolted out of bed and woke up Janelle beside him. "Get your clothes on. We've got a problem."

She tried to see him in the dark, with sleep-clouded eyes.

He leaned over and kissed her hard. "Wake up, now."

She shuddered and bolted to the dresser, throwing on a T-shirt and jeans as fast as he did.

And then he smelled it. "Jeez, this is not the way I wanted this evening to go."

She didn't understand, and he regretted what was about to happen next. Pocketing his phone, he headed to the top of the stairs, his hand holding hers. Downstairs, he heard something. He called out, "Evan?"

"Yeah, I'm trying to get through the damn doors. Come

and give me a hand, will you."

They raced down the stairs and realized all the doors had been bolted from the outside.

She stared at them in confusion. "I don't understand."

"You will soon," Evan declared, his tone hard.

And suddenly one window, then another, and then another all shattered, as things were thrown inside.

She stared in shock and horror, when suddenly the rooms were engulfed in flames. "Oh my God," she shrieked.

Guilliam grabbed her and wrapped towels around her face and yelled, "Get down to the floor and stay with me."

He ran, with all three of them racing from one room to the other. They headed for the French doors, and Evan backed up, then plowed forward, literally throwing that heavy weight of his body through the glass door and onto the patio outside. The smoke was black, with flames licking away at the walls of the structure, quickly climbing up the sides of the house, already lapping at the roof. They couldn't hear any sirens.

Guilliam noted her bare feet and picked her up in his arms and said, "Hang on tight."

She wrapped her arms tightly around him, as he stepped through the glass door out into the blackness of the night, now lit up by the horrific flickering flames that shone all around them. The noise of the fire was deafening too. As he raced away from the property, Evan grabbed his arm, directing him.

"This way," he cried out.

Still stumbling from the smoke, their mouths covered, he was directed through another yard into another space. Once there, they all stopped. Guilliam gasped for breath, pulling the cloth down from his face, and crying out, "Did you see him?"

Evan shook his head grimly. "I'll leave you two here. I'm going out on the prowl." And, with that, he was gone.

Guilliam slowly lowered her to her feet, pulling the towel off her face. Leaning her over, he said, "Cough to empty out your lungs and fill them up with fresh air," he murmured.

He did the same, even as he looked around in the distance. Now he heard sirens on the way.

She looked up at him in horror. "My mother's house."

Guilliam nodded. "I know," he whispered, the sorrow evident in his tone. "I'm so sorry."

She just blinked at him, and he realized she wasn't processing what this would mean to her. He hoped it didn't mean as much as he suspected it would. She'd lost so much already that losing her mother's house and everything in it would be a heavy blow. With this fire, no way anything would be salvageable either. His main concern right now was whoever had set off the fire.

Then a voice behind him spoke in a snarky tone. "Look at that. You got out of there. That's just too damn bad because now I will have to do this myself."

Guilliam turned around and saw a stranger staring at him, holding a gun.

"Why do you have to do it at all?" Janelle whispered, looking at him. "Haven't I been through enough?"

"I don't care what you've been through," he muttered. "You're just making my life really hard."

"*So sorry about that,*" she snapped. "*Not.* I'm getting awfully tired of assholes screwing up my life."

He snorted, raised his gun, and replied, "I don't give a shit, but I don't need the headaches that you keep presenting.”

“Yeah? And what headaches are those?” Guilliam asked, watching Evan closing the distance behind their gunman. “I don’t understand what you’ve got to do with any of this.”

He shrugged. “And you won’t. That’s just the joy of it, right? There’s always got to be that extra little twist. And you can bet that the old man knew exactly how to make those twists happen,” he told them, nodding.

“So, who are you?” Janelle asked. “The illegitimate child or just one more of many hired hitmen who the old coot thought he would need.”

The man laughed. “Do I look like a kid?”

“In the darkness, I can’t tell, but maybe.”

A dark, almost growling sound came from him. “Just keep that shit up,” he warned, but then he laughed. “Not bad though. You just sit there, crying, trying to find some way out of this scenario. That’s about as good as I can expect from you.”

Guilliam pointed out, “She just lost her mother and was kidnapped, and now you’ve just burned down her house, her mother’s home, so every single possession either of them had is now gone.”

The man stopped for a moment, then turned to her. “You had a shitty day.”

“Ya think?” she snapped, her tone caustic. “And more than that, I’m damn tired of assholes like you controlling my life,” she muttered.

“Yeah, well, when you get mixed up with assholes like this, things are bound to happen.”

“Assholes like the old man?” she asked. “Why do people keep getting mixed up with that old guy? I just don’t see why someone would. So I need somebody to explain.”

"It's called being friends with the wrong people."

She shook her head. "I don't even know who you are."

"No, you don't, and that's a good thing."

At that, an odd sound came from behind their gunman.

He turned and motioned at Evan. "Just in case you think I didn't see you, get your ass over here."

Evan stepped forward and glared at him.

"Oh, look at that face. You don't seem happy. You're a fucking investigator. That's who you are." But this time he had turned to eye Guilliam. "And that bloody Jasper. Apparently he just stepped in and took over, didn't he?"

"Jasper?" Guilliam repeated.

The gunman shrugged, as if suddenly aware that his identity might become something they could guess at. "It doesn't matter."

Guilliam replied, "If it doesn't matter, then tell me because I don't understand. I've met Jasper, and, yeah, he's taken over the investigation department, but what difference does that make to you?"

"It doesn't make any difference," he said smoothly.

"Apparently it does."

Then Janelle added, "Unless you're one of the old investigators."

A moment of ugly silence passed, and then he snorted. "I'm not sure who the hell you think you are, but you better keep that mouth of yours shut."

She nodded. "That's it, isn't it? You're one of the former investigators. That's how the old man kept tabs on what was happening on the base. You're the one he had in the hole, the mole—the one guy who could get access to information Greg's granddad needed, who could give access to information needed for blackmail. That's how the old man got a hold of everybody, so he could twist their arms and force them to do this shit," she cried out in a fury.

The gun pointed in her direction.

She nodded. "Yeah, so maybe I will die right here. I've already been in that situation not all that long ago, and I don't even know how many goddamn times, and that's just today," she yelled at him. "But now I find out that you're supposed to be one of the good guys, you're supposed to be one of the men in that navy department that looks to solve these crimes? How many criminals have you given a free pass to over the years, *huh?*"

He shrugged. "A couple, but only if they had the money."

"So, freedom was something that you charged for, depending on what their bank account looked like, didn't you? And you probably had access to those balances, so you could determine exactly what that amount would be." Janelle stared at him in shock. "Have you no shame? Does your mother know what you're up to?"

He snorted at that, as Guilliam grabbed her arm and whispered, "Easy."

She glared at him. "No, I won't take it easy. Do you realize what that means to somebody like me? Somebody who believes in law and order, who believes in right over wrong, who believes in good against evil. Then you find out that a piece of shit like this guy is out there, playing his own little games, killing people, letting criminals off, blackmailing innocent people. And why is that?" she asked. She turned and looked at Guilliam. "So, how come you haven't met this guy yet?"

"Because," he replied, looking at the gunman, "you're Steve, the investigator who's off on medical leave, right?"

The other man gave him a small smile. "Yeah, nice to meet you. Glad I missed all that fun stuff with Morgan. You probably thought Sam was guilty, didn't you?"

"We cleared him of any wrongdoing today," he shared, "but, yeah, his attitude sucks. So I was hoping he was guilty. I wanted to smack that man across the mouth a time or two."

"I'm sure you did," Steve agreed, with a laugh. "As it turns out, he's one of the good guys. It's just, he, … he's got mannerisms that make you want to kill him anyway. … You don't know how many times I wanted to kill that miserable fucker. As for Morgan, I knew he was on the take, but I didn't understand how deep he'd slid."

Steve looked over at Janelle and sneered. "You just keep believing in all those lies, those fallacies. We need people like you around. We can take advantage of the gullible ones like you," Steve shared, "and you're right there with them." He shook his head at that.

"And what is your relationship to the asshole behind all this?" she asked, staring at him. "There's got to be something. Have you been helping Greg, the grandson, or just keeping watch and taking care of your own little sideline blackmail business on the side?"

"Both," Steve said. "Keeping track of the last-standing grandson because he's generally okay at what he does. However, he has one focus and one focus only, and that's entirely money-oriented. The minute you get that happening, you get all kinds of little shits changing the rules to fit whatever it is they want to have happen," he shared, with a laugh. "And that doesn't work out so well for the old man."

At the phrase, *old man*, Guilliam studied him, figuring out what was driving Steve. In the distance, the roar of the fire crackled, lighting up the sky with bright orange and yellow hues. Sirens filled the air, and Guilliam knew the firemen were working hard to stop the fire from spreading to every other corner of the neighborhood. "So, you had to torch her house, didn't you?"

"You were all supposed to be in it," he noted, with a sad smile and a mocking expression in his eyes. "It would have been so much easier."

"You should have shot us first then," she stated, sneering at him. "Because now there's no way you can cover this shit up. Three bodies, all at once, in the neighbor's backyard? That won't be so easy to hide."

"Shut the fuck up," he snapped. "Besides, I might have somebody helping me," he added, with a laugh. "So, we'll just take you all away from here."

"Yeah? Dead or alive?" she asked.

The gun was cocked and pointed at her again.

"If I'm dying tonight anyway, I might as well go out with a fight. If I'm a prisoner, that's my right, isn't it? I'm supposed to fight back, aren't I? I'm supposed to make your life miserable," she declared, glaring at him.

Guilliam wasn't sure where she got such spitfire bravado from, but, as he well knew, it came up at odd and inconvenient times, particularly when she was riled. Right now, she was riled. He motioned at her to step off to the side, but she refused.

"Nope, I will stay right here," she argued, standing in front of Guilliam. "You shoot me, and you probably shoot through both of us."

"You're right," Steve agreed.

"And then what will you do?"

"I'll use the third guy here, the big one, to carry your

bodies to the vehicle."

She glared at him. "Wow, you're an asshole, aren't you?"

"Yeah, I am," he admitted, with a laugh.

Then he flicked the gun in the direction of Evan, who had taken one step forward. "I wouldn't do that if I were you."

She shifted forward and turned to Evan. "Yeah, Evan, you're the big heavy guy, so you've got the job of carrying our dead bodies." While Steve was glaring at Evan, and Evan was glaring at him, she quickly took several steps forward and kicked the gun in his hand. It didn't come free, but it knocked him off balance, and both Evan and Guilliam jumped Steve. Evan body-checked and dropped Steve, just like Evan had plowed through her beautiful French doors. The gunman didn't move. She walked closer, then crouched to see if he was still alive.

"Hey, I'm not *heavy*," Evan corrected in a mild tone. "I'm muscled."

She grinned at him. "Yeah? Tell that to my French doors."

He patted his tummy. "I'm not heavy. I'm fit."

She smiled. "So I don't have to share grub with you ever again?"

"In that case it was worth it." He looked down at Steve and back over at Guilliam. "So, this guy?"

"No, I don't know him," Guilliam shared, as he stared down at the man on the ground. "But, when Jasper took over the department, one of the original team members was off on medical leave. I thought his name was Steve, so I took a chance."

"Which it appears to be," she pointed out.

He nodded, then pulled out his phone. "Now at least we

have somebody else to grill."

"Do you think it's over?" she asked.

He looked over at her and frowned. "What do you think?"

She sighed. "I don't know. There's just something about this, something I can't quite place."

Both men turned instantly to her, and she shrugged. "I don't know what it is, but something's nagging at me."

"Great," Evan muttered. "That whole *there's something but I don't know what it is* just isn't helpful." She glared at him, but he smiled. "I agree with you on that. Something else is definitely going on."

She rolled her eyes. "I can't believe what a shitty day this has been." As she turned to look back at her house, she didn't even know what to say.

"I'm sorry," Guilliam whispered. "Losing your mother's home on top of losing her has got to be about too much to take."

The way he said it just made everything hurt that much more. She nodded. "I could look at it that way, or I can look at it as granting my mother some peace. I won't be hanging onto any remnants of the last three years. I do have some special mementos and things that I had in storage because I was looking at selling the house and moving on," she murmured. "And I guess this is exactly the time to do that."

"It sounds like it to me," Evan said. "Nothing is salvageable here."

"I see that." She looked down at the clothes she wore. "Before we go anywhere today, I will need a change of clothes."

"I think we all do," Evan agreed.

Both men were in jeans but had no shirts on. She asked,

"What about the vehicles? Do you think any of ours survived the fire?"

"Yours was in the garage," Guilliam noted.

"Oh, crap," she muttered. "So, in other words, not mine."

"Exactly," Evan replied. "Ours, however, should be okay."

"Great. That's something at least." Janelle shook her head.

They waited until Jasper arrived, and it wasn't long before he came around to the backyard where they still stood guard over their prisoner.

Jasper frowned at them and asked, "Are you all right?"

"Sure," Janelle said. "I'm just struggling to keep the bitterness out of my tone. This was my mother's house."

"Oh crap," he muttered, as he turned to look at the charred smoking remains behind them. "It went up so fast." He looked over at his men, and both nodded.

Evan explained, "He bolted the doors from the outside, then threw multiple Molotov cocktails into the house. It went up instantly."

Jasper groaned. "At least we've got one more asshole to interrogate." Jasper turned on his flashlight and pointed it at the prisoner. He nodded. "When you told me who it probably was, I had to go look it up in the files. Sam is still as obnoxious as ever. Lichen just got back from holiday. They are all culpable as far as I'm concerned. It's time to clean house."

"Good thing you have your own team in process," Janelle said.

"They are shocked over this news too."

"That'll be interesting for the new investigative team to

interrogate the old investigative team," she noted. "I'm hoping that won't involve me."

"It shouldn't," Jasper stated, looking at her. "I'm not sure what to say or what to tell you to do now though."

"She's coming home with me," Guilliam declared. "We need to go shopping and grab a few items. She's lost everything, which also means she'll need to deal with insurance, et cetera," Guilliam warned.

She winced. "I am so tired of this shit."

"I suppose you had a little bit to say to Steve," Jasper noted, with a wry smile.

She glared at him. "Yeah, and I would have had a whole lot more to say if I thought anybody would listen," she muttered. "But apparently nobody's listening to me these days."

Guilliam just chuckled.

The prisoner sat up. He glared at everybody but stayed quiet.

Jasper nodded. "Good idea, Steve. Just stay quiet. We don't want to even think about talking to you right now."

Steve shrugged. "You won't get anything out of me anyway."

Jasper laughed. "You would be surprised. Everybody says that shit to us. Then the next thing we know, they're all trying to make a deal, once they realize they won't see daylight for another twenty years."

Steve shrugged. "I highly doubt that's the case."

"Of course not," Jasper quipped, as he marched Steve forward, heading for the MPs, who had just arrived.

Guilliam turned to Janelle and opened his arms. She raced into them. He held her close, as the rest of the men walked away, giving them privacy.

"Is it over?" she asked.

"I hope so." He frowned. "We can't be sure just yet. It still seems unfinished, but that could just be me still looking for bad guys when there aren't any."

She tilted her head back, frowning at him.

He smiled. "Let's go. We need rest. We'll sort the rest out tomorrow."

"The rest? Like us and our relationship?"

"Nope. Nothing left to sort out there," he whispered. "You're exactly where you belong."

Her gaze warmed, as she stared up at him. "Are you sure?"

"I was always sure. Sometimes the timing just doesn't work out, but now hopefully, for us, it will."

"I'm so—"

He placed a finger against her lips. "No. No more apologizing. We're here together now. And the future is ours. Now let's go enjoy it." He released her, and she held out her hand.

"Together ..." she repeated.

Guilliam laughed and interlaced their fingers. "From now on ... always."

This concludes Book 5 of Man Down: Guilliam.
Read about Mason's Mark: Man Down, Book 6

Man Down: Mason's Mark (Book #6)

There is no greater motive than bloodlust, DNA, and revenge mixed up in a cocktail of hatred ...

Grateful to be alive, Mason knows he owes his friends and family not only for his life but for protecting his wife and unborn child. When he realizes that it might not be completely over, he's on guard, yet not capable enough to defend his family, so he must rely on those around him.

Tesla can't believe it's over. Mason will make it. They have gotten to the bottom of who targeted him and why, ... right? It's over surely. Until Janelle calls in a panic, crying out a warning, and Tesla realizes to what extent deep pockets, empty promises, and the vow of revenge can drive one person.

Tesla will do anything to keep her family whole and safe. No one—and she means *no one*—will take that from her now ...

GUILLIAM AND JANELLE headed to his car, walking past the remnants of her mother's house. Janelle stopped and stared, feeling the tears well up in her eyes. Yet resolutely she turned and walked away. She caught sight of the gun-toting arsonist, stooping to get into the back of a cruiser. Something about the angle of his face, the expression on his face, got her attention. She froze, not exactly sure why it seemed familiar.

Beside her, Guilliam nudged her and said, "Come on. It's over. We can buy you a change of clothing, then go home, get a shower, clean up, and maybe grab a few more hours of sleep." As they neared his vehicle, the other team members were gathered there—Masters, Gideon, Evan, and Jasper.

Janelle shook her head. "I won't sleep now."

Evan snorted. "Yeah, neither will I." He faced Guilliam and said, "I think I'll just head out, if you guys are okay with that, unless you think you need me still." He turned to look at each man, then at Guilliam again. All the men shook their heads.

"Wait," she called out, then frowned. "I know this will sound horribly strange, but—"

"But what?" Jasper asked.

"Evan, would you do me a favor?"

"Sure. What is it?"

"Go to the hospital. Something doesn't feel right …" She stumbled over the words.

All the men stopped to face her. "Why?" asked Jasper.

"I don't know. I'm hoping it'll come to me, but just

something is there."

Evan nodded. "I wanted to check in with Tesla anyway. I'll grab a change of clothes and head over to the hospital. Will that work?"

She nodded and smiled. "Thank you."

"That's okay. You just owe me another meal." And, with that, he took off, chortling to himself.

She looked over at Guilliam, as he helped her to his car. "I like your friends," she shared, with a big smile.

He smiled back at her. "Good, but they're also *your* friends. You've known both Evan and Tesla for a long time. You've met some more good people here, and they will love you just as much as I do."

She shook her head. "Even knowing what I did?"

"Of course. Nobody judges you for looking after your mother."

"Just me," she whispered.

"And you shouldn't either," he stated. "Now come on. Let's get you home. We will have a boatload of hassles to deal with, considering we just lost our wallets and anything else you might have had in your purse that just went up in flames. Luckily I do have some cash at home."

She winced at that. "God, my ID, credit cards, everything," she muttered, reality dawning.

"Yep, I know, but it's not the end of the world."

"No, it isn't," she agreed, as she got into the vehicle. She reached for his hand and added, "Not exactly the night I thought we were having."

"No," he said, with a big grin. "Still, we survived yet again, and now it's over."

She nodded, took a deep breath, and whispered, "Is it?"

He asked, "Will you be okay with your house—"

As they drove past her house, she sighed and then nodded. "I think so."

"You only think so?"

"It'll probably take a little bit for it to settle in."

They drove to his home first, so each could get changed out of their smoke-smelling clothes. He gave her one of his T-shirts and a pair of shorts, plus flip-flops, way too big, but she had nothing on her feet otherwise. This would do until they got to the store.

As she headed back out to the car, so they could do some shopping for necessities for her, she turned and added, "There's still one thing bugging me."

"Okay. What is that?"

"I don't know," she cried out, "and that's why it's just driving me nuts."

He hesitated. "And you're sure it's important?"

"Yeah, it's very important, but I don't know why, and I don't know what."

"Okay, just think about it while we drive."

She sat back, closed her eyes, and tried to relax. Her life had been a shitshow for hours now, and, as they drove, she thought about the ups and downs of her day. And then it hit her. "Oh my God." Her eyes flew wide open. "It's not over. It's not. Turn this car around. We have to get to the hospital right now."

He stared at her in shock but hit the brakes, already navigating a U-turn. "What do you mean?"

"There will be another attack on Mason and Tesla. I'm sure of it. We need to go. Go, go, go."

And, with that, he went silent and focused on speeding toward the hospital. Once they were headed in the right direction, he asked, "Do you want to explain what this is all about?"

She could barely talk. "Call them. Call them now."

He snatched his phone as they drove to the hospital at hell-bent speeds, punched the last number called, and put the phone on Speaker.

When Evan answered, he asked, "What's going on?"

"Are you at the hospital?" Janelle yelled into the phone.

"Not yet. Why?"

Guilliam replied, "Janelle's in a full-on panic, and we're heading there now."

"Okay," Evan said in a slow tone. "I don't have a problem heading up there right now. I told her that I was going to."

"Yeah, apparently she recognized something."

"Yes," she yelled again. "His face, ... her face, ... the nurse who didn't like me making tea. They have similar features ... Get there, Evan, please! Now!"

Find Book 6 here!

To find out more visit Dale Mayer's website.

https://geni.us/DMSMDMasonsM

Author's Note

Thank you for reading Guilliam: Man Down, Book 5! If you enjoyed the book, please take a moment and leave a short review.

Dear reader,

I love to hear from readers, and you can contact me at my website: www.dalemayer.com or at my Facebook author page. To be informed of new releases and special offers, sign up for my newsletter or follow me on BookBub. And if you are interested in joining Dale Mayer's Reader Group, here is the Facebook sign up page.
http://geni.us/DaleMayerFBGroup

Cheers,
Dale Mayer

About the Author

Dale Mayer is a *USA Today* best-selling author, best known for her SEALs military romances, her Psychic Visions series, and her Lovely Lethal Garden cozy series. Her contemporary romances are raw and full of passion and emotion (Broken But … Mending, Hathaway House series). Her thrillers will keep you guessing (Kate Morgan, By Death series), and her romantic comedies will keep you giggling (*It's a Dog's Life*, a stand-alone novella; and the Broken Protocols series, starring Charming Marvin, the cat).

Dale honors the stories that come to her—and some of them are crazy, break all the rules and cross multiple genres!

To go with her fiction, she also writes nonfiction in many different fields, with books available on résumé writing, companion gardening, and the US mortgage system. All her books are available in print and ebook format.

Connect with Dale Mayer Online

Dale's Website – www.dalemayer.com
Twitter – @DaleMayer
Facebook Page – geni.us/DaleMayerFBFanPage
Facebook Group – geni.us/DaleMayerFBGroup
BookBub – geni.us/DaleMayerBookbub
Instagram – geni.us/DaleMayerInstagram
Goodreads – geni.us/DaleMayerGoodreads
Newsletter – geni.us/DaleNews